MW00569432

A PIG IN PARIS

A Pig in Paris

Stories

Steven Huff

Big Pencil Press 2008

Big Pencil Press, Rochester, NY 2008

Copyright 2008 by Steven Huff
All rights reserved
Manufactured in the United States

First Edition

ISBN 13: 978-0-9819018-1-7
Big Pencil Press

For Betsy

Contents

Part III: Wild

Acknowledgments

About the Author

Part I:

It Has Come to This

Paris

HE WOKE WHEN he heard singing. Blinking and gazing around the dark hotel room, he realized the voices were far away, barely louder than his wife snoring beside him. Yet they had roused him because there was something familiar in the melody. As he listened the voices came closer, louder, intermingled with a horn that did not accompany the song so much as dodged and sparred with it. The song was in his own language, the first English he'd heard in the three nights they'd been in Paris, except for the conversations he'd had with his wife.

He slipped out of bed. Now he knew what they were singing: "Hello, Magic Woman." He opened the door to the balcony, and watched the singers stumbling down the winding street, half a dozen boozy boys, one blowing on a trombone. Another leading a large pig on a leash. They were butchering the song.

"Hey," he hollered as they passed below. "I wrote that song. Be careful with it."

Only the pig looked up at him. But in Paris one hardly notices a man standing on a balcony in his underwear.

He went back into the room where his wife still slept (it had been a long day of struggling with the language and menus; ennui had set in, and they had both had a lot of wine). He grabbed his robe from a chair and ran down the stairs to the street, walking quickly in the direction the boys had gone. He passed a number of people, but they paid him no notice. In Paris it is not remarkable for a man to run down the street in his bathrobe, because men there are always chasing something at night.

On the Rue Trois Freres he spotted the boys and the pig, and he bolted after them as if they had stolen his wallet, although all they had was his song, and everyone in the Western world had that song. It was his only hit, which he'd recorded long ago when garage bands still had a shot at recording contracts. It had made him briefly rich. But, whatever magic he had possessed vanished after that recording, and he had soon found himself with an ordinary office job, a house and family, a potbelly, and a tired sallow complexion. But in America it is not remarkable to be suddenly famous, and just as suddenly forgotten, the way the first astronauts entered space for a few minutes before falling into the ocean and going back to work.

One learns to shut up about it.

The boys and the pig entered a cafe. Happy shouts came from inside, as if the crowd had been waiting for something exactly like these boys and the pig. He stood outside looking in at them singing in the midst of the crowd: *Hello magic woman, with the streetlight in your eye, lay down with me softly...* Damn them, they were farting it up with that trombone.

He went in, and stood near the door. Now the boys began singing his song in French, and the crowd sang along dreamily and drunkenly. But since he could not speak the language, he could not join in.

A waiter approached and spoke to him in French. And he answered, "Uh, *no parlez vous...*"

So the waiter responded brokenly, "Do you... want...something?"

"That's my song," he told the waiter, pointing at the boys. "I wrote that song."

The waiter shook his head as if he didn't understand in the din. So he repeated himself, whereupon the waiter turned and waved another waiter over to him. "He says that is his pig," the first waiter said the other.

"No, no, no, I said nothing of the kind! I only said that I wrote that song."

The other waiter held up his finger, signaling him to wait. And he came back in a minute with the pig on the leash.

"Hey, hold on here," he shouted as he was pushed out the door with the squealing animal. The crowd laughed and the boys hollered *au revoir* to the pig. And the waiters told him—in suddenly perfect English—never to bring the pig in there again or they would call the police.

He walked back toward his hotel with the leash in one hand and a half bottle of Cote Roti in the other that someone in the cafe had gleefully shoved into the pocket of his robe. He sang his song to the pig now, and he sang it right:

Hello magic woman, with the streetlights in your eyes, lay beside me softly....

"I wrote that song," he told the pig. "I recorded it with Asylum Records thirty years ago. Before your time, I guess. It made number ten on the Billboard Charts, and I even sang it on the second-to-the-last *Ed Sullivan Show*."

In America, or almost anywhere else, he would have been in trouble. But in Paris, for a woman to come to the window and see her husband on the street below in his bathrobe, with a pig on a leash, singing. Well, these things happen.

Orbits

THE AMERICAN PROFESSOR spoke Russian like most foreigners. As they sat in the cafe he said things he didn't realize he was saying, and sometimes it was very funny, or very stupid. Although she laughed, she wasn't sure how close she wanted to get to a man who could discuss only the most mundane things in her language. He smiled awkwardly whenever she found what he said so hilarious. But how long can one laugh at such things? She got up and left the cafe, but he followed her.

His short, red beard was speckled with gray. Probably a bit older than she. Of course he didn't struggle up eight flights of stairs with her, with half a litre of vodka in his belly, only to sit in her tiny apartment and drink her lousy tea and listen to a symphony on her record player. He wanted an adventure, she knew. Maybe he thought it would be his last before he finally had to accept old age, and all the usual infirmities waiting to mug him like the roughs in Moscow's streets.

He looked unsettled and puzzled when she said, "I have a husband." He gazed around her apartment as if wondering if he had misunderstood her, since there were no signs of a male here among her decorations and sweet wall art, no burly coat hanging on a peg, no work shoes in the corner. Nor had there been any signs of a man in a very long time. "He is in orbit," she continued, pointing upward with her thumb. Then she told him the rest of the awful story. She supposed it was safe to tell; things were different in Russia now. Yet, even if things weren't different, he may not have understood anyway. He settled back in his chair squinting as if squeezing his brain to make it function better.

Then he was truly startled when she suddenly stood and pulled her blouse off over her head. She wasn't young— he must see that. But her small breasts were still firm and only a few strings of her short hair were gray. His glasses nearly fell off as she tugged him to his feet. Such a funny man. So this was what American professors were like.

In America they probably didn't climb long flights of stairs and have to stop on the landings to regain their breath. They took elevators. And immigrants waited on them and made their tea, and turned their beds back. Their women did not live in the same small apartment for decades, going to work like everyone else while their husbands were on long space missions.

After things had changed in Russia, the government and all the rest, she had read something that an American astronaut had said to reporters. He had said that he had seen an old Soviet capsule in space, still orbiting—for God knew how many years. And he had said there was a cosmonaut inside it. *Really?* people had said, shocked. Could it be true? Soviets had never said anything about those first flights until they were over and the cosmonauts were safely home. But if a flight was never over, if it never came down, then they would say nothing publicly about it. She believed it was true, and that it was him. Or was it him? Maybe there were others. She had to believe it was him, and that he had died quickly, that his radio had not transmitted a fading voice pleading for impossible help, becoming at last an intermittent beep in the vast dark.

In her bed the professor kept looking over his shoulder, though not actually twisting himself, as if he really hadn't understood what she had told him, and expected to hear heavy feet on the stairs, a big Russian man to come in the apartment and kill him. Or perhaps it was only that he too had someone, some woman lost in the vast darkness behind him, in America or somewhere else, whose voice still orbited his thoughts and startled him sometimes.

Indeed, there were many feet on the stairs—it was an apartment building after all—tromping up and down until he finally relaxed. He began talking again, saying things by mistake. But it wasn't as funny in the dark. As they lay side by side, looking up as though they could see into space, he asked, "When will your husband come down from orbit?"

So, he had not understood. Stupid man.

She said, "In two thousand years, maybe more. His capsule will fall into the ocean and sink to the bottom. And then I'll be free. In the meantime, please, go to sleep."

The Shadow of Hollywood

BILLY MILO'S CAREER in Hollywood was a long one. He'd worked with almost every big star from Chaplin to Marilyn to Nicholson, playing bit parts in more than two hundred and eighty movies: westerns, comedies, sandal-epics, cloak-and-daggers, and tear-jerkers. And now he was on his deathbed. His family gathered at the hospital, but Billy waved away the young priest who came to perform last rites. "Tell him to come back tomorrow," Billy cranked. He was dying all right, but not quite ready.

Billy wasn't kidding himself. He knew his passage wouldn't make the smallest ripple in the tinsel kingdom, but not because he wasn't successful. Indeed, those films added up to regular work for fifty years, although almost no one in the industry knew that, save himself and his agent, Bert Smiley. Billy Milo was an unknown because, in every single movie he acted in, his bit parts ended up on the cutting room floor. More than two-hundred-eighty times.

Any time he'd explained that fact to anyone he had to pause a moment to let it sink in, so absurd did it sound. Because, even in an industry where studios waste untold millions of dollars, waste careers and lives without a blink, where they buy rights to fifty novels for every one that's ever produced, where veteran screen writers sell one script after another to studios which only shelve them—even in that atmosphere, Billy's career was unusual, and probably a record. Two hundred eighty—ah, why bother counting?

"But dear," his wife Ardis pleaded at his bedside, "Father Kelly has been here all morning."

"Ha!" Billy's veins popped red all over his forehead and bald pate like a map of LA freeways. "Trying to cut me out of my last role, is he? Tell him the Shadow still lives."

The Shadow of Hollywood. That was his nickname among his friends, folks who loved to watch Billy's old flicks and who made a game of looking for his shadow which many times was left inadvertently in the films. His only lasting contribution: a little shaded light.

"I want to see Bert first," Billy drawled weakly. "Get my agent in here."

Ardis sighed, and picked up the phone.

When Bert came in, he expected Billy to say goodbye. And Billy did, sort of. But he also had a request.

"Find out if anybody needs a stiff," he told Bert.

Bert thought Billy had gone off his bean. "A stiff? You mean a body?"

"That's what I said. See if anybody's in production who needs a dead man. I mean soon. I can use the work."

As a matter of fact, Bert did know of one. And early the next morning Billy's lifeless corpse was lying in full dress on a table in Studio B. The director, Lawrence Kasdan, called for a series of overhead close-ups of a woman's hands dressing a dead man as if he were going out for the evening, simulating an undertaker's finishing touches for a movie they hadn't named yet, *The Big*...something. That morning they dressed and redressed Billy fifty-seven times trying to get it right. But Billy didn't get tired of it because Billy was dead.

"Don't shoot his head," Kasdan hollered. "He's supposed to be young, a thirty-something suicide."

But it was during the rushes, after the morning's shooting, when the director and cast watched the scene over and over, that they realized something wasn't right.

"What's wrong with this picture?" Kasden hollered.

"I'll tell you what," said a young actor, leaning against the wall. "He's too old."

"But," Kasden retorted, "we must have put five pounds of makeup on his hands."

Five pounds wasn't enough

"Okay," Kasden yelled. "Let's shoot it again." Then he turned and hollered to the young actor still leaning against the wall, "Costner, yank the clothes off that body, put them on yourself, and lay down on that table."

Kasden was already striding out of the room when he turned and hollered again to the crew, "And send that body back to Bert."

Come, Let Us Die

A CROWD FOLLOWED Jim Bolton out of the lecture hall and into the street, jostling him so hard he almost dropped his books in a puddle. It seemed that these people wanted to squeeze him until he grunted one more line of poetry, press him to sign one more copy of his book. It was too much, this sudden attention, this new manna of notoriety. His host hailed a cab for him. And as he climbed into the back seat along with his new friend (though he couldn't remember her name), his host gave him a pat on the back. "We'll see you there," he said.

Bolton nodded and smiled wearily. Then the cab door closed with the playing of the usual recorded message which one must always endure in New York City taxis—but this time in a brogue deep as the East River: "Hello, this is Dylan Thomas. Remember to fasten your seatbelt."

He looked at his new friend (was her name Felicia?), "Did you hear that?" he asked.

"Where to?" interrupted the driver.

"567 Hudson," he said, "the White Horse Tavern."

Well, had she heard that voice? he asked again. But she said she hadn't. And Bolton snorted. So, the city was cooking up another gratuitous PR scheme? Just when you think you've heard the silliest things imaginable, they get someone with a brogue to impersonate Dylan. Usually the voice was Beverly Sills or Mel Torme, or someone else of that ilk, telling you to buckle up. But this!

As they pulled up in front of the White Horse, the host was already out of his own taxi and waiting on the curb for Bolton. As he opened the door, the voice came again. "This is Dylan Thomas. Before you go into your good night, get a receipt from the driver and remember to take your belongings."

"Did you hear that?" he said to his host as he climbed out of the car.

"What do you mean?"

Bolton sputtered, pushing his glasses up on his nose, and hiking his trousers up on his lanky butt. "Oh... some Welsh imposter. Never mind."

He didn't really need more drinks. What he really wanted was time alone with his lovely new friend. But one doesn't often win a Pulitzer. And he couldn't refuse a round at the fabled White Horse—where admirers crowded his table—nor the several rounds that followed. But, when the party finally broke up, Felicia (or Felicity? Velocity maybe?), had wandered away. Bolton said goodbye to his host, then waited sullenly at the bar to see if she would come out of the ladies room. He finally stumbled out to the curb alone.

Another taxi. And again the recorded advice, "We're going to drive your green age anywhere it wants to go," the Welshman's voice came again. "But first, fasten your seat belt."

This was someone's idea of a prank. Probably Harry Hartmill's, whom everyone had favored to win this year. In fact, people were shocked when Bolton had won, and said so a little too loudly. Hartmill must have hired some bad actor to drive him nuts— that's what this was. But then, how did he manage to involve so many taxis? Maybe Hartmill should have won it. It would serve him right. Did he think it was easy or fun to be dragged by one leg through all this madness, shuttled from city to burg, not remembering what hotel he was in, much less where he'd left his suitcase?

"Stop right here," Bolton shouted. The cab skidded in the rain. He threw money over the seat and dashed from the taxi before he heard the end of: "I am dumb to tell a hanging man, remember to get a receipt..."

He downed two fast scotches in an Eighth Ave. bar, then dashed to the sidewalk again and hailed another cab. As he climbed in, the same voice called on him to buckle up. But this time he'd had enough. "I don't care who you are," Bolton shrieked. "You never won the Pulitzer Prize."

Startled, the driver looked back at him.

But the bard's voice came calmly, "That prize, my good fellow, only goes to Americans."

"Ha!"

"Nor did I very much care," added the bard.

Bolton saw the driver waving to a passing patrol car. But he couldn't help it. This business had to be settled.

"You were a drunk!" Bolton yelled. "Worse than me, by far!"

"Perhaps," said the bard, "but my women never abandoned me."

In the back of the patrol car, and breathing easier, Bolton watched the street zipping by. When they stopped in traffic on MacDougall, he saw a pedestrian peeking curiously at him, as he had often done himself—stolen looks at people riding in the back of cop cars. It was irresistible. And how he'd always envied those young dogs their adventures: to ride, to be taken away from everything. Of course, when you get to the station it becomes quite a different experience. But the ride, the ride was the prize.

" 'Dilly, dilly, come let us die,' " Bolton chirped.

And one of the cops glanced back with that look cops wear when they know they've done right by arresting a man; like a fisherman looks at a particularly bizarre and awful fish that he's caught, like maybe he's just done the river a favor.

The Museum of Natural Futures

WE WERE IN Washington on our honeymoon, and we went to the Museum of Natural Futures. The first thing we did, Missy and me, was sit together in a machine that read our blood pressures, listened to our tickers, asked where we lived, our birth dates, what we did for a living, and what kind of food we ate. Did we smoke, did we drink, did we shake extra salt. It would tell us our natural future together—biological and medical probabilities; of course, no certainties. But the more solid info we gave it the more accurately it could prognosticate. This machine was like a little space capsule that flew us into a galaxy of data, a Hubble Telescope on our advanced years. I inserted my credit card before we climbed in, and it charged me $39.95 for the Deluxe Extensive Analysis. By the time we'd buckled into our seats, it had already x-rayed our lungs, CT-scanned our brains, recorded our weight, checked our optic nerves, and looked in our ears.

The museum is a dark building on Constitution Ave., one that gets a lion's share of the funding cuts, which is probably why most of the interior lights are unlit. More people seem to come out than go in because most get right up to the door, buy their tickets, and then chicken out. Well, you can't blame them. Most of the exhibits are about global warming, coastal flooding, extinctions, ozone depletion, and avian flu. And then there is this machine to make it all feel personal. You get plenty bad news for free, why pay for more? We even said that to each other. But we went ahead all the same.

The voice that asked the questions had the flat tone of a machine's voice, yet it seemed to make *Hmmmm* sounds from time to time, or maybe that was just the machine stirring its porridge of data. But the long silences that followed some of our answers were *not* my imagination. And I didn't dream the *cluck-cluck* sounds after we'd revealed our previous addresses, former occupations, and whether we were first-born, last- or middle-children, adult children of boozers, offspring of depressives, if our grandmothers bit their nails, whatever. We were told to breathe hard into a little tube to test our pulmonary health. It sent us to the restroom one by one for urine samples which we were instructed to pour into a little hatch in the machine that looked like the top of a Mr. Coffee reservoir. The voice commented on Missy's eczema, and on her bunions (which it had noted without her taking her shoes off), and on my varicose veins and sciatica.

Then the voice told me, "Your lungs look like an ashtray."

"Wait a minute," I said, "I quit smoking at age thirty-five, and that was ten years ago." Silence. I added, "I take vitamins and I exercise three times a week." That was a lie, of course—I'm lucky to get one workout, plus a few Sunday pushups. But I fibbed because I was getting hot under the collar: I was paying $39.95 to have my day spoiled.

"Do you have any hobbies?" the machine asked.

"Yeah," I said, "I collect Chinese postage—"

"I am addressing your wife."

"Yes," Missy said, "I collect doll wigs."

Then the machine spoke candidly to Missy. It explained to her that, whether I knew it or not, I had lived on top of a chemical dump from 1978 until 1997 (during my first marriage), that I was therefore saturated with dioxin, mercury, and significant noxious other stuff—that I was toxic—and that she should consider leaving me. Above all, she should not sleep with me or let me do it even with a rubber. While I was sitting right there, it said this stuff. It was like that moment you reach in marriage counseling when the shrink and your spouse have decided mutually that you're not present anymore and begin talking to each other as if you'd fallen through a trap door.

I barely remember the rest of the museum, our stroll through the Halls of Future Coastlines, Climatology, Flora, Fauna, and Viruses, scenarios that I didn't give a damn about if Missy was going to take the machine's advise and leave me. Of course I did not want to ask her what she'd decided. How could I ask such a question on our honeymoon? Why did we have to come to Washington for our honeymoon? How stupid. What was the matter with the Pocono Mountains? Or why didn't we just tour the Capitol, or the White House, or Ford's Theater, or the Department of Labor? Why didn't we go to the Naval Museum and look at the pickled brain of Leon Czolgosz?

At lunch we had oysters, and I nearly got up the courage to ask Missy. It was like the fear I felt when I asked her to marry me. And it occurred to me then that she had never said yes. I could not recall her ever having said it. I only remember her saying that she would think about it. She said yes to the preacher of course, but that is not the same as saying it to me. Yet somehow, we had planned our wedding and done it without actually agreeing. So, she would be unlikely to give me an answer now, a real one.

"Missy," I said. And she raised her eyebrows expectantly. But I couldn't ask. Instead, I said, "How are your bunions?"

Story's End

WE USED TO hang out of the hay window of the Good's barn and drop firecrackers on the chickens in the yard below. I mean, when we were kids we did that. It's a wonder we didn't burn the barn down. The chickens were too stupid to get out of the way, so they got their toes blown off, and so forth. This was all part of growing up. Kids tend to straighten out eventually, or at least I did.

Keith Lennihan, one of us kids, is a muscle-bound village cop now, and a bachelor. Tommy Miller became a driver for a movie director out in California. And Chappy Good is still a toe-headed farmer. Lennihan is called Toughie now, and late one Friday night he chased a woman speeder clear to the Canadian border. Toughie clocked her at ninety miles an hour, which is really hauling in a Volkswagen Rabbitt. She'd have gotten away, but she ran out of gas right in sight of Customs. Her bad luck. She had her kid in the car with her, a little boy, and that made Toughie mad, endangering an innocent kid. So he brought them back to town and locked the mom up and took her kid over to his sister's house, who's an ex-nun, until Family Services could take him.

His sister opened her door in her nightgown, and he shoved this squalling kid at her. She hollered, "What the devil is this?" And they got in a big row right there at her door. Toughie has a laugh that sounds like a fist full of little rocks clacking together, and part of what burned his sister up was that rocky laugh as he walked back to his patrol car.

Now, you probably think you know where this story is going, that Toughie is going to marry the girl he threw in the slammer. But, no.

Anyway, his sister—Ruth Lennihan—gave the kid some cocoa, and listened to his tale of whoa about how he and his mom were coming home from the grocery store minding their own business, when Toughie started riding their bumper and spooking them, and one thing led to another till his mom freaked out and tromped on it. So, Ruth went down to the station the next morning with her own money to bale the woman out. Naturally she didn't want to leave a lone young woman in a cell with only her brother to guard her. But the mom had already been arraigned and bale set at ten thousand bucks.

For the past couple years Ruth had worked on the village road crew as a flagger, though once in awhile they'd give her a shovel and let her throw some gravel around. Never mind that she closely resembled her brother and could have picked up the rear end of a Skiploader. But she didn't have ten thousand bucks. Not many ex-nuns do, if you think about it. But she figured she had another card up her sleeve. She took the kid out to the Good farm that afternoon—Chappy himself was running it now, and I was helping him out on Saturdays—and she gave us the whole sad story.

I have to backtrack now, and also make a point. Passions run high in this little burg. When you feel passionate about something in a small town where there isn't a whole lot else to do or feel, it can take over your life. Like God ringing your doorbell. Anyway, that was how Ruth had felt when she'd fallen in love with Chappy Good back in high school; but he'd dumped her for a pixie blonde, and Ruth was so busted up over it that she was a nun for ten years before she realized what a chump he'd been and didn't deserve her love in the first place. Back then a predictable percentage of girls went into the convent, and people forgot about them; so everybody was shocked when one of them came back. Like she'd returned from the dead with a mission to make us all nervous. But anyway, going out to Chappy's farm wasn't easy for Ruth. Even after all those years.

Chappy was shocked to see her. But he didn't have any money either. Neither did I, sorry to say, but we sat down and cried with the little kid, snapped his suspenders, and said, "Keep your chin up." I think it would be fair to say that Chappy and I have both become sensitive men. And the kid was cute. Then we got on the blower to Tommy out in Hollywood, who happened to be sitting in the parking lot of some swanky bar when he got the call on his satellite phone. The movie director was in the bar at the time eating lunch with some big starlet, and Tommy was waiting for him.

We took turns talking to Tommy, and he hollers,

"My man!" and "Ruthie baby!" And he sounded just like the old Tommy.

He didn't have any money either. I guess even the satellite phone belonged to the movie director. But he cried too. Then we gave the phone to the kid so he could talk to a driver for a real movie director, waiting in the parking lot for a real starlet. And pretty soon the kid was smiling. It was the first time our whole gang had talked together—minus Toughie, of course—in years.

You probably thought you knew how this story was going to end, with us getting the kid's mom out of jail. But no. There wasn't a damned thing we could do for her.

Sick as a Dog

O'FARRELL WAS ON the kitchen phone talking to his new doctor, reciting his symptoms. His elbows were on the table and he shook salt distractedly into an empty coffee cup. He couldn't get this doctor's name right. It was something like Rajamanda. Or, maybe Rajavaneda. No, that wasn't it either. Earlier he'd talked on the phone with the secretary who repeated her new boss's name about fifteen times, and he still didn't get it. To make things worse, the new doctor's accent was impossible, a barrier of garbled-sounding words like a glass wall that he couldn't hear through clearly. And it was serious. This Raja-something might be telling him—in that confounding accent— that he was going to die, and it would go right past him. And now the secretary, Janine, whom he'd known for years, had started acting like she couldn't understand O'Farrell's brogue, just to put him in his place or something.

What the hell was going on in that office? Old sympathetic Dr. Dillet had retired two months before. And now there was Raja, telling him over the phone that his symptoms didn't add up. Or that's what it sounded like. "Did I hear you say my symptoms don't add up?" O'Farrell sputtered.

"Yes." Raja replied. "I say, taken all together, they make no *since*."

O'Farrell figured he was saying, no *sense*. He wanted to say, Look, I've been sick longer than you've been a doctor, as if feeling like hell for fifteen years had conferred a kind of honorary degree. After all, he knew what he knew: He felt like crap. Old Dr. McManus back in Sligo, Ireland, never a very friendly man, nevertheless did not quiz the people who came to him sick. Dr. McManus assumed you weren't making it up when you said you were sick.

But Dr. Raja wanted more details before ordering more tests, especially since O'Farrell's file was already two inches thick with old tests for the same complaints, none of them proving anything in particular. "Tell me how your stomach now feels," Raja said.

"Ah, well, I feel like—" O'Farrell turned to look at his wife Bridget drinking tea at the table, as if he expected her to come up with the description the doctor wanted. Under the table lay Butler, his old springer spaniel, so decrepit his bones creaked like a wheelbarrow when he walked. The sight of that dog's suffering broke O'Farrell's heart. Sooner or later he would have to drive Butler to the vet and have him put down. Though he wasn't sure that the dog was worse off than himself. "Sick as a dog, I am," O'Farrell told the doctor flatly.

Dr. Raja sighed, and mumbled something.

"What was that now?" O'Farrell asked.

"I said, I need stool *simple* and urine *simple*."

After stopping by the doctor's office to pick up the sterile vials, O'Farrell took Butler for a walk. Having Butler on a leash struck him as a useless ritual; the old dog could no more run away than climb a telephone pole. O'Farrell was running out of patience for useless formalities, for professional silence. Why couldn't they simply check him into the hospital? No one told him anything anymore. Or they said it fast, with their backs to him, and refused to repeat it. Or they said it in an exotic accent. Medicine was becoming more scientific, and more cabalistic. Damn them all. Or as his mother would have said, "Damn them by bell, book, and candle light."

Janine the nurse had given him a clipped answer when he'd asked her what sort of tests they were going to do on his piss and shit. "Urine cytology," she snorted, "and they'll probably look for blood in your stool. And a whole bunch of other stuff. Now have these vials back to us by four o'clock, or you'll have to do them all over again."

He went over that encounter several times in his mind as he walked the dog. He would like to plant a microphone in Raja's office to find out what he was really saying about him. He would like them to find an ugly tumor in his stomach the size of a fist—something operable, mind you, but scary. Something that would tear itself out of his body, like that *Alien* movie, and chase Raja and Janine down the hall and over the far hills. O'Farrell burped, and the dog burped. Then the dog halted, coughed.

He hoped his stool—whenever he managed to produce it— proved so full of disease that they would have to wear space suits when they examined it.

Butler whimpered worriedly. They'd walked too far while O'Farrell mulled his problems. It was going to be hell for the old mutt to get back home. Then the dog steered himself toward the grass, and squatted painfully. A shadow of pain always crossed the dog's face when he pooped that made O'Farrell tense. The hound could drop dead at a moment such as this.

"Gets harder all the time, don't it, old pup? Sure, and I know how you feel."

Then, as he watched the dog straining, he suddenly had an idea. Hmmm, he thought. He reached into his coat pocket for the vials, and broke their protective seals, and bent to the sad dog.

"*Go raibh maith agat,*" he thanked the dog in Gaelic as he scooped a bit of turd into the larger cup. And a few minutes later he bent and caught the dog's stream in the other vial, adding gratefully, "*Go raibh maith agat, sa!* This should do it, old dog. This will make them sit up and take notice."

And it seemed as if the dog laughed.

Island Goats

THE VACATION HAD taken a sour turn. Mike tried to imagine that it was just that he and Lorenne weren't used to so much togetherness. How much can a man and woman be alone together before their nerves grate? It's only natural, isn't it? But he feared the trouble was deeper than that. The arguments had been about children: their children, who didn't exist yet, children he wasn't sure he wanted to exist. At least not as sure as Lorenne was. All Mike knew was that he didn't want to spend vacation arguing about it, or discussing the traumas of his own childhood where he suspected the roots of his misgivings were hidden.

When he woke this morning he didn't wait for breakfast, but took his tackle and a thermos of coffee down to the boat, started the Evinrude, and turned the bow toward the fog. All morning he cast and reeled, long after the sun had burned the fog away. He hadn't been out in the boat all week, and now he was doing all his fishing at once.

Then, sometime after the sun peaked, he realized how hungry he was, and far from shore. He hadn't caught any fish; he'd have to make up a story when he returned to work, something about catching a pike or a muskie but letting it go.

Heading for shore, he kept Merwine Hill in his sights. The cabin he and Lorenne had rented was between that hill and the shore. But the odd thing he noticed when he neared shore was goats grazing on the slope. And there were no docks, only a rugged shore. Mike realized he wasn't at the mainland at all, but one of the little islands that had dotted the map that he'd spread on the cabin table under the Coleman lantern the night before.

Maybe this was Copper Island. About two acres large.

He waded ashore and pulled the boat up on the sand, then walked toward two cabins on a high knoll while the goats shied away from him. Someone must be around. He could get a drink of water, maybe—he hated the taste of lake water. And maybe he could get directions to the Grand Marina Cabins where he was headed. But most of all, he would satisfy his curiosity about this island.

He got no answer when he knocked on the door of the shuttered first cottage, nor at the second, although the windows weren't shuttered there and he peeked through the glass. He saw a table with plates and cups, a messy surface as if people had gotten up abruptly from a meal and gone away, never to return. Mike walked around the buildings and around a little pole barn looking for a pump, but found nothing and his thirst was mounting.

He went back to his boat, thinking about bringing Lorenne here. *You've got to see this place,* he heard himself telling her. It looked almost like they could move in and pick up where the mysterious other people had left off.

He could imagine her saying, *And live on what, goats?*

Yes, on goats. What else? And he laughed, looking at the herd which had run to the shore to watch him sail for the mainland.

But, once again, he didn't recognize the mainland shore when he approached it. Was this another blasted island? But it looked like Merwine Hill right above the shore. This had to be the place. Where was his rented dock with the blue tie-up post for Cabin 7? He turned east and buzzed along the shore for a mile, and didn't find his dock. So he turned west. This is crazy, he thought.

Then, up ahead, he saw people gathered on a dock, maybe half a dozen men and women in bathing suits waving and calling to him. Nothing there looked familiar either, but maybe he could ask directions. He approached slowly and when he came within fifty yards he saw they were not men and women, but children. Calling, beckoning. Well, then, adults must be nearby, someone who could set him straight.

The first stone that flew into the boat hit his tackle box. He still wasn't aware of what was happening when the second hit his leg. Laughter came from the children on the dock, and they sent more stones flying at him.

"Hey, what the hell are you doing?" he hollered, shocked. But they only sent more volleys of stones, striking Mike in the chest and neck. As he reached for the steering arm, one stone hit his nose and broke it like a wishbone.

Mike spun around and roared back out into the lake, one hand over his face running with blood, as he zig-zagged toward the horizon.

Latch

THE MAN WHO would one day be known as Latch
was born Alain LaChance, one of fourteen children in a
French-speaking family in central Quebec. Arrested fifty-
one times by his sixteenth birthday. In fact, he got arrested on his birthday; and this time they locked him up for
good—or until someone, a judge or a priest, could figure
out what to do with him. It happened that a Canadian ex-
boxer-turned-holy-roller, named Hard-Neck Schutz, had
decided that the best way to handle young savages like
Alain LaChance was to put them in the ring, and let them
get the hell beat out of them, then talk salvation into their
busted heads. Reform school gladiators. Authorities were
offended at Hard-Neck's gall, but were ready to try anything on the bored, drunken brats who were filling their
rural jails. And Hard-Neck had case studies, documented
cases of boys who were transformed.

But Alain didn't reform. When he put on the gloves
he beat the spuds out of every Quebec kid that came his
way, and soon was Whelp-Weight Champion (a category
invented by Hard-Neck himself for his kid fighters) for

all central Quebec, and was punching his way south. He became Lash LaChance on posters. His average opponent fell in three rounds.

It was 1959, the end of the first decade of TV, and when these Christian boxers finally got a slot on Canadian prime time, the public thought they were going to see a polite version of the awe-inspiring Friday night fights that Gillette broadcasted from Madison Square Garden down in the states where, usually, two black men whaled the hell out of each other. But this was Canada, and these were *young* boys, Christians at that. Maybe they'd raise a bloody lip at the worst. However, when Ragin' Roy Hawkins from Windsor, Ontario faced Lash LaChance, people in living rooms all over Canada jumped to their feet in horror; Lash bashed that kid until he lay splattered like an upended casserole.

Switchboards jammed at CBC. People wanted the head of Hard-Neck Schutz, who himself went after Lash in the locker room as soon as the boy stepped out of his shower. He'd told the kid before the fight to cool it down. "This is TV, you little Frog," he'd said. "You gotta be nice." But Lash had seen his big chance to be noticed by a real promoter; to hell with Schutz and his Jesus fights for hamburgers and Cokes. Now the ruined Schutz whipped Lash LaChance all over the locker room with his belt.

Lash couldn't seem to land a punch on tough old Hard-Neck, and so he got whipped bad, and kicked out into the night alone with only a towel around his butt. For weeks he roamed Montreal, shop-lifting, living by his wits.

It was now clear to Lash that fists were a thing of

the past, same as horses and butter churns. You had to get automated. He acquired a gun. And soon he was swiping TVs left and right. He became known as Latch LaChance for his lock-picking prowess. Latch had never learned good English, but he knew what his new name meant. In those days TVs were heavy buggers. But they fetched a good buck if you didn't drop them down somebody's stairs. It was a hard life, dangerous as a rattlesnake farm. But for the first time Latch felt free.

One night he was on the English-speaking side of the city and he went into a dark apartment where he was pretty sure no one was home. But inside he heard the unmistakable voice of that big-time American TV preacher, the one that filled all the stadiums. He crept ahead and saw an old woman asleep in an overstuffed chair with her mouth hanging open; or at least she seemed to be sleeping. Latch laid his head on her breast and couldn't hear the slightest breath. He sighed and crossed himself; then reaching over he changed the channel. It was time for the fights. It was round three of a match between a tough Newfy and a Quebecois, beating each other to mush. Blood running, teeth jarred loose. What a battle. Latch whooped.

He heard a clicking sound, and turned to see the old woman roused in her chair. She'd picked up the gun he'd carelessly set on her coffee table when he'd thought she was dead, and now she was sighting him along the barrel. "Turn that channel back!" she said.

Latch sort of understood, but he was excited. He pointed at the boxers on the screen. "I fought too," he said in French. "I was like them. A fighter!"

The old woman pulled back the hammer. "Turn it back to Billy Graham."

So, Latch thought. It has come to this.

Where Snow Comes From

THE BIG TIRES of the bus from Albany rocked against the curb at the Schenectady terminal. The driver zipped his coat before getting off to take tickets. Glennie, in Row 8, watched the trickle of passengers thumping up the stairwell with snow on their shoulders and hats, scanning for seats in the low light. She avoided eye contact with them, so not to idly invite anyone to take the spare seat beside her. None looked like anyone she wanted to ride next to for two-hundred-plus miles. Then she stiffened when she saw the old man who brought up the rear of the group.

Later she'd ponder how her recognition of him had been almost instantaneous. God, she hadn't seen him since—hell, how old had she been then, eight or nine? If she'd thought about him at all anymore, she'd assumed he was dead. But this lean man dropping his bag on a seat across the aisle, one row ahead—traveling with an old woman, fetid odors radiating from both—was her father. She put her face in her hands for a moment, and looked again. A lot of men on buses looked like him, rough and unshaved, but she knew him because his coat was open at the neck, and there was that old red sun on his throat.

It was a scar, actually, where a doctor had done a hurry-up tracheotomy when her father was a kid with the croup, and had done a sloppy job at that. But when she was little she'd believed—because someone had told her—that the red sun on his throat was the spot where God had touched him one night when he'd knelt before the whole Assembly of God congregation to be healed of booze. Cured of all its stink and rapture. Throat, thirst no more. When she was little she liked to touch the spot that God had touched, and it had sent a lovely frisson up her finger.

She would know his throat anywhere, even now clustered in wrinkles.

The weather was horrible. Back on the Thruway, the bus churned along behind a plow that also spread sand. The trip would be long.

For awhile, Glennie only looked at the rough cut of her father's hair, and the old woman's head, whoever she was, and at the collar of his plaid wool coat. She imagined him going into a store and picking that coat, taking money out of his pocket—maybe a bundle of cash tied in a handkerchief—and paying for it. Maybe, since he looked so beaten-down and tired, he'd bought it figuring on it being his last coat, the coat that would see him through.

Slowly, and almost apart from herself, she got up. She teetered on her feet for a moment as the bus rocked, unsure of what she was going to do next. The floor was slick from snow tracked on board. She squatted next to his seat. He gave her a befuddled look, as did the woman beside him. Two bewildered faces in their last coats.

"Dad," Glennie said. Her feet were cold and it hurt to squat there.

His eyes crossed as she spoke again, and then he grabbed her right hand in both of his. "Rita," came his old voice; familiar but rougher. "Rita."

"No," she said. "Rita was my mother. I'm Glennie, your daughter." Booze so saturated his body that his flesh itself was booze. If she touched a match to him he might burn like a flambe. As much as she was made of burritos and chicken and Pepsi, he was made of booze.

She knew other people had to be listening, and it made her neck crawl. But there was no going back to her seat now. Hell with those nosy people.

"Rita." He squeezed her hand.

"Dad, I'm Glennie. Mom has been dead for four years. Well, longer actually. I'm going to Buffalo. My boyfriend lives there, and I'm gonna—" But she didn't finish because she was focusing on his red sun. Pink, really, though the overhead light gave it momentary other colors. She wondered how she'd ever let herself be kidded into believing that story about God reaching his finger, like in the Michelangelo ceiling, but touching a drunk's throat.

The old woman butted in. She said, "John, let go of her and face the front." She even yanked his hands from Glennie's. But he grabbed Glennie's hand again and squeezed it like a trap.

He said, "I can't talk so good no more, Rita. I'm losing my voice."

The hem of her coat was soaking in the melt-water

on the floor. Her feet were going to sleep. Glancing ahead, she could see the part in the driver's hair in his rearview mirror, and he occasionally peeked back at her.

The bus rolled into Utica, the lights of the town fanning the dim interior of the bus, and a few people reached for their bags. Her chance to end this. Glennie stood up. "I've got to get off here." She pulled herself away and reached for her bag in the overhead rack.

Her father looked puzzled, but smiled. She knew he was waving as she hurried off the bus, but she didn't turn around. And moments later she was standing in the snowfall outside the Utica terminal, the air even colder than she remembered in Albany, only about fifty miles ago. Then the bus was gone. Now what the hell? she thought. Now what the holy hell? She walked up the street half a block, but she wasn't sure what she was looking for, so she walked back to the terminal.

Inside, she talked to the ticket agent. Then she found a payphone near the doors, and dropped her bag on the floor. She could smell her father's hands on hers as she dropped coins into the phone. She would have to find someplace to wash, or else try not to care about the smell.

Gary answered on the fourth ring. Where was she, he asked sleepily.

"You won't believe what just happened. I ran into my father on the bus, or what's left of him, I guess."

"Huh? You're kidding me."

"No. Why would I kid you? He was on the bus holding my hand—and he looked, like, dazzlingly lost. And I didn't know how to deal with it, so I just got off.

That's why I'm calling. I'm at the Utica terminal and I guess there aren't anymore busses tonight."

Gary gasped. He was awake now; she could even hear his bed springs as he sat up. "Jesus, Glennie. So, what are you going to do? Where are you going to stay?" She heard his voice rising from bewilderment to exasperation, reminding her of a kettle starting to whistle.

"I don't know," she said. "Kind of . . . on my own, I guess."

"Look, I'm coming out there, right now."

"No!"

"Of course I am. You're stuck."

"I'm not stuck, Gary, I'm safe. It'd take you hours to get here from Buffalo, and it's snowing like hell—"

Then it was as if he looked out the window and saw the weather. And the pitch of his voice fell again when he said, "Okay."

"Okay," she repeated, looking beyond the phone at the empty terminal.

"What are you going to do?"

"I'll do something. Good night." Then she added, "Damn it," before she'd quite set the phone on the hook. And she thought Gary might have heard it. She stood and waited to find out if he'd press *66 to get the number, and call her back. She waited until she felt stupid for waiting.

Frost crept up the door glass. No one passed on the street. The question came to her, where the hell does snow come from? Not sure I was paying attention that day in school when they explained that. From outer space, maybe, and a huge killer storm could come at us, same as a comet can hit the earth, and we'll be buried and all memory gone. No, that's stupid. Snow comes from out on the ocean or the Klondike or someplace. God, I'm losing my head already.

Glennie went into the ladies' room, and washed her hands. But as she dried them she was struck by sudden remorse, and she sniffed her fingers, but her father was gone. She stared at herself for a long time in the mirror. Then she took her lipstick from her purse. Carefully, she drew a small red sun in the cleft at the bottom of her throat. Working carefully, she made the sun larger, radiating.

Odd how her father's sun still glowed in the dull folds of his old neck. Like his eyes. Well, old drunks' eyes often glow, sort of watery. Not to say, even—how do you say it? *Beatific?* That was it. That church word she remembered from long ago. Shaking her head, she soaked a paper towel in hot water and wiped the sun away.

Where the hell had he been going tonight, anyway? It hadn't occurred to her to ask when she was with him on the bus. All she knew was, it wasn't where she was getting off. That was for damned sure. That had always been for damned sure.

The Z Train

THE TUNNELS I drive in are dark as hell's shit house. And I'm the only light running on the track, driving the Z Train underground like a lightning bug flying through the intestines of a big beast. And just as much a secret. I'll tell you, I've been driving this train a long time, and I know every crack in the tunnel, every old paper cup lying by the rails for years. Shortest train in the whole subway system, with the fewest passengers.

I had a passenger one night, crazy as a rat on D-Con, busted through the panel behind me, barged into the cabin, and threw himself on his knees next to my seat, screaming, "Help me, for God's sake!"

I didn't know what the hell to do. I'm not trained to do anything but drive. So, I just kept my eyes on the tracks, on the tunnel in front of me, figuring this dude would be taken care of soon enough. His clothes were expensive, light charcoal suit, but he was all ruffled up.

He kept screaming, "Can't you hear me?" I tried not to let on how bad he was shaking me up. I just kept driving.

Incidents like that on the Z are pretty rare. In fact, in twenty-seven years, that was the only bad night I've ever had. See, the Z runs the whole length of Manhattan, all the way up the west side, and back down the east before crossing under the river into Brooklyn and back around. You've never heard of the Z because you're not supposed to hear about it, and I'm supposed to keep my mouth shut. I run in the *old* subway tunnels, ones that are officially closed. And that's why I often see bums down there that have found their way onto the old dark and closed down station platforms where they've set up their little camps. Even the train itself is a vintage you haven't seen since the late fifties. Noisy, shakes like a wet dog. There aren't any working stations, only a door in a tunnel wall here and there where people get on and off. Certain people, I mean, usually in suits. Once in a while you see some kind of foreigners in orange jumpers and leg irons. Sometimes nobody at all—last Christmas Eve I drove my whole ten-hour shift without picking up a single goddamned soul.

Now, these dudes that were riding when this man broke into my cabin, they'd got on the Z down at Wall Street through one of those little doors in the wall. I'd got a signal to stop there, and the little door swung open and these suits got on. Nothing unusual until we got almost up to Harlem where that crazy dude swung into action.

But, like I expected, it didn't last long. Another dude in a suit came into the cabin through the busted door, and said something calm and collected, like, "Pardon me, sir." To me he said that, not to the man on his knees. I just nodded to him, and kept my trap shut while he reached down and grabbed that dude on the floor by his necktie and hauled him to his feet.

Then he said to me, "We'll be stopping at Door 9." And he dragged that man back to his seat in the car. But the panel was busted open now, and I had to listen to him scream and carry on for most of a half hour. About being innocent. Meant no harm. And on and on until I was half nuts.

Door 9 is under the East River, right about in the middle. Just another single door like all the others, painted green with a yellow light over it. When you stop there you see old phone and telegraph wires hanging in bunches from the ceiling, old pipes dripping. It gives me the spooks to stop there—especially that time, watching them take that crazy mother off and through the door. Screaming his lungs out.

Wall Street to Door 9. Goodbye.

If you're ever waiting for the A or C Train down on West 4th, or the 4, 5, or 6 on 110th, or waiting for one of the trains at Jay or High Street out in Brooklyn, or in a dozen other places, you might hear a train come in and rattle to a stop, and when you look up from your newspaper, you rub your eyes because there isn't any freakin' train. Not on your track, or the track on the other side. That's because it's the Z, and it's on the other side of the wall. That's why it sounds a little muffled. And if it's at night, it's probably me, pulling up to one of those little doors. Same old track, same old dark.

Part II:

The Asylum of History

The Book Proposal from Hell

DEAR EDITOR,

I want to write a book about Hell: its past, present, outlook for the future, and about its realities as opposed to common misconceptions. You see, Hell has changed, utterly transformed from the horrible place you've read about in scripture, heard from preachers, and probably envisioned in your guilty dreams. I've been in Hell for many years, and I'm highly qualified to write about it. In fact, I'm the first soul to receive an official imprimatur from the Devil Himself to write a book about Hell. However, no onus was placed upon me by the Lord of Darkness to brighten its realities in any way.

But first, some history. It may interest you to learn that there is an aristocracy in Hell, which is one of the things I like least about it—that, and the criteria for inclusion in the upper castes of the netherworld. Although in rare instances we stand in whithering awe at the descent to our realm of some monumental sinners—need I mention any one of them?—the prevailing aristocracy is one of antiquity. At the very top of the social heap are those early few who came down to us around the time of the fratricidal Cain, some six thousand years ago, followed soon by the Sodomites. Another early immigration was the Pharaoh's army which arrived enmasse about thirty-five hundred years ago, dripping wet.

You may rightly assume that all languages are spoken here; however, certain tongues have predominated at different periods. There were the plague years when a cacophony of European languages swept through Hell like a new Babel. During the late eighteenth century French became so predominant that signage had to be altered to prevent them from seceding and starting a Hell of their own. During 1861-65, American English began to take over, and "Aura Lee" became a popular song.

But the greatest changes in Hell occurred more recently when a collection of history's radicals and rebels, including Spartacus, Leon Trotsky, and Joe Hill organized the masses of the damned and stormed the Satanic Citadels, winning important reforms, including a fresh carbonated water supply, beer on Tuesdays, and temperatures reduced by as much as 7,777 degrees. Hell isn't much toastier now than a sauna bath. These changes, however, only raised the noses of the aristocracy. They remember when Hell was Hell. And so on.

Other transformations have been more gradual. Ever since the invention of Purgatory, Hell has been losing ground. It isn't the destination it used to be. Now it is mainly the worst, the die-hard unrepentant who come, sort of like the maximum-lock-up monsters in your own state prison system. The quality of the damned is certainly changing.

As for the Devil Himself, old "Beelzebub," He's giving me an opportunity I never had when I was alive: the chance to become a published author. That is, of course, if you have the good sense to give me a contract. I can provide photos, latest statistics, and my personal reminiscences of some of the baddest dudes in history. Come on, damn it, give me a chance.

You may reach me by phone at my temporary earth address for the term of this project.

Yours Truly,

Steven Huff

PS: On second thought, don't contact me. I will come to you. Don't be upset—I promise my visit will be pleasant.

The King's Taster

THE MOST TERRIBLE thing has happened at Court. The King's food taster was found dead. Long live the King! But the news was a shock. Dear old Charlie, who had been King William's food sampler, grog sipper, candy nibbler, tobacco puffer, snuff sniffer, and medicine sampler, standing valiantly between William and any possibility of poisoning since the time when he was a boy-prince, expired mysteriously about half an hour after the King himself finished his mid-day meal. In fact, it was the King who discovered him when he went out to the drawing room after his feast for a smoke by the fire and found Charlie sitting in a chair, uncharacteristically unresponsive.

One would assume that any poison in the Royal lunch would have taken prompt effect on the taster, well before the King himself took his first bite. But Charlie had wandered out here, where he sat, dead but still warm. Was he the victim of some insidious slow-working poison? The King rang his alarm bell frantically, summoning his aids, including myself; and I called for the Court physician who put his ear to Charlie's chest and confirmed what we all knew by then.

It was difficult to guess what distressed the King most—the loss of his oldest friend, or the possibility that whatever killed Charlie was creeping through his own intestines. Well, I suppose I am being sycophantic. It was most assuredly the latter, because William ordered the physician to do an immediate autopsy while also—immediately!—preparing and administering a mustard-and-vinegar emetic to the King. He ordered the entire kitchen staff arrested, as well as the huntsman who had provided the fowl, and...well, he couldn't think of anyone else to arrest just then.

"On with the autopsy!" he gurgled as he hurled his lunch into the royal latrine. "Oh, uh...arrest my tobacconist. And my vinter."

Now, Charlie was elderly and, to be frank, his own doctor had warned him to stay away from fat and sugar and wine and tobacco and peculiar mushrooms, and all that manner of substances that it was his responsibility to swallow and snort and smoke so that, if he survived, the King could enjoy the same with impunity. Charlie knew he needed to retire from this awful job, and he had confided his doctor's advice to the King's jester, hoping that he would explain to the sovereign in a jovial way what Charlie couldn't tell him in a serious manner because the King would only slap his taster on the back and say, "Nonsense, old boy, you're as fit as any young hound that ever chased a fox." In desperation he'd even approached several of the King's mistresses, hoping they would weave the message into pillow talk. But no luck.

And now Charlie was being sliced open on a table, the cooks were chained to a wall, and the King was, well, in the latrine howling and attempting to squat and kneel at the same time.

It was while his Highness was so indisposed that the physician, a certain Mercado, a Spaniard and reputedly the greatest man of medicine in Europe, summoned me to the room behind his office where he performed surgeries. I entered with a deep foreboding, and holding my nose as surgeries on the deceased are never pleasant. And there lay our Charlie under a dangling lamp, his chest open like a folio revealing his ravaged organs.

"You must inform the King," Mercado said. Indeed, he hardly needed to point out any peculiar cause of death. Both lungs looked like charred logs, his heart looked like a fist full of headcheese, and his open stomach displayed a mass of ulcers.

I threw my hands in the air. "Tell the King what?"

"There is clear evidence of poisoning," he stated flatly.

"Poisoning! My dear man, I'm no doctor, but I can see that this fellow has simply done his job too well. That he died so well should be a bellwether for the King to moderate his own diet."

The doctor washed his hands in a basin and dried them on Charlie's old coat. "Diet?" he squinted at me.

"Yes," I said, following him through the doors to the stairs that led up to the King's chambers. "Overeating. Too much drink, too many sweets."

Mercado stopped on the stairs, and turned to me. "All those things you mentioned are good for you. Peasants get no surfeit of them, and they're lucky if they see the age of forty. Besides, would you have the King drink the water in this kingdom?"

"No! But no one needs three gallons of wine every day to quench his thirst. Poor Charlie had only the first glass from each bottle, and look at his liver."

The doctor's stare told me that I was talking my way into suspicion, so I shut up. Yes, I swear, I kept my tongue lest I lose my entire head. And, as the King's scribe, I even wrote the terse death warrants that sent the cooks, the poor hunter, and several others to the gallows. And further, to erase any possible suspicion of myself, I have become the King's taster.

You can only imagine the things I eat prepared by his new cooks from the continent: snails, the liver of the bird of paradise, flamingo tongue, frog eggs on toasted bread points, the tripe of bear, and I must say more wine that I can easily swallow. I feel very unwell. Not that that has gained the notice of the King, since, as soon as I have swallowed some base and ugly thing, and have not died from doing so, he digs into his plate with a vengeance, burping about his victory over the treachery of his former cooks. When I have drunk the wine, he clinks his full glass against mine and another bottle is opened. And another. And I swear I am being poisoned.

Professor Langley's Study

IN PROFESSOR JOHN Langley's family there was an old story about an uncle who was a train engineer in the steam locomotive age. As the tale went, this engineer named Albert Langley was running freight one night from Pittsburg to Philadelphia at full throttle. As the train ascended a long curving grade through the woods, he saw the light of another train approaching on the single track. Startled, he braked and yanked the whistle, dragging his train to a stop only a hundred yards from where the other train also halted. Something was very wrong here. His train was scheduled for this track; no train should have been coming the other way. Albert waited, catching his breath (he had been ready to jump), but there was no movement from the other train. So, he and the fireman got off with a lantern and walked toward the other engine. They got close enough to read the number on the engine, 1129, when its breaks released with a whoosh and it began backing away, slowly, until it disappeared around the bend. Crazy behavior, he thought.

He shrugged and went back to his train and began chugging forward again. If they were going to follow a reversing train it would be a long trip; they'd never get up to full speed until they got to a town where the other train could switch to a side track. But, as they rounded one bend after another, there was no other train in sight. A plain impossibility. How fast could that other train have backed up? They reached Philadelphia at daybreak, and Albert checked the schedule. He found that there had been no mistake in scheduling, no other train was supposed to be on that track in that region at that hour. Moreover, he was told, no train had carried that number, 1129, for more than twenty years. In fact it was the number of a train that had plunged into a river when a bridge had given way. He must have been mistaken, a manager impugned—or delusional; or, more likely, he was making up the story to cover for some unscheduled stop. At a whorehouse, maybe.

The story always intrigued Prof. Langley. He didn't believe in ghosts, but he believed in his uncle's subjective experience—that is, regardless of what had actually occurred (God only knew), he didn't doubt that Uncle Albert was telling the truth as he had perceived it. Albert had died when Langley was too young to question him about it, but the whole family believed that he had seen something. And the fireman corroborated Albert's tale, which made it harder to refute.

It also interested Langley because he loved trains, almost more than anything else. As a kid he'd had multiple train sets crisscrossing the family's attic. As an adult he'd ridden trains throughout America, Europe, and Patagonia, and he'd even ridden the Orient Express. When he married Carol they'd honeymooned on a train through the Canadian Rockies to Vancouver, and though she wasn't as enamored of the train as he—she'd wanted a trip to Acapulco—they'd had a reasonably good time.

"Trains," he'd explained to Carol, patiently, "are... well, they're almost on an astral plain. You pass through a place, and you are there, but you are never *of* the place. You can even see through house windows briefly at private lives. But you are really apart from them. You watch, and imagine, and go on. And you can never, never be bored."

His favorite American author was Thomas Wolfe for stories like "The Far and the Near," about the hapless engineer who left his train and tried to become a part of the lives of two women who lived along the track and who had been waving to him for years. And for the scenes in *Of Time and the River* in which Eugene Gant rides a train along the Hudson and longs for a life in the grand houses he sees along the river. He longed to teach those books to a class. To stand in front of a class and rhapsodize on the poetic ironies in the story of the engineer who finally approached those women who backed away from him, and who felt violated by his sudden intrusion.

Langley was actually a specialist in the classics—especially Homer and Sophocles—but he wondered how long he could hold out in that arena. During a decade and a half of teaching he'd watched his full classes flag in popularity until only an odd minion of graduate students remained, with hair as haggardly cut as his own, and with that blaze of dreamy urgency in their eyes that the study requires. But there were no longer enough of them. He had another interest in collecting American folklore and tall tales, a long-time hobby that began claiming more of his time after he began studying yarns about ghost vehicles, like his uncle's train story. Of course, lurking behind his interest was the kindling of an idea to develop new courses at the college that would include the study of folktales, even contemporary urban legends. If he could come up with something that made sense to the department, it might save him when the last of his own dreamy kindred had vanished from the study of Homer. If. *If.* So far no one was listening to him.

But ads that he placed in *The New York Review of Books* and a couple other publications, seeking stories, brought a flurry of phone calls. "Tell Daddy there's another screwball on the phone for him," Carol would tell one of the kids after the phone rang.

It was hard work. And without a real goal, other than to simply collect stories, and to ponder what to do with them all. Sometimes when Carol talked to him he could not help noticing that her eyes would fall on his beard, its increasing wooliness, its animus, and her voice would trail off; and her topic, whatever it was, about their bank accounts or whatever, would be dropped with a comment like, "It's late, John, do you want a Cognac?"

No, he wouldn't want a Cognac. So she would drink his Cognac as well as hers.

* * *

Carefully searching oral sources, doing hundreds of interviews, Langley found that many families had similar yarns about ghostly vehicles: a truck that backed away from a one-lane bridge to let a car through, only to vanish on the other side; an old touring car that drove into the long driveway of a farm and sat there until the family finally came out to see who it was, whereupon it backed out and drove away. Of course there were thematic variations, such as a mysterious carriage that passed a house in the night just as a family member died. And a much more common tale: the traveler who saw a car in his rearview mirror following closely on a long road, only to look moments later and see that—impossibly—it had gone. Also, the vanishing Jesus-like hitchhiker. But his family's story remained unique in that it was about a train. Somewhere in all of it, he believed, was some common thread.

He became "Vanishing Jesus" at department meetings, for his own disappearances: one minute pouring himself a cup of coffee and seeming to settle down for the meeting, the next minute sneaking back to his desk to phone someone back who had a spooky story.

At the neglect of practically everything else in his life, including his family, his house, his beard, his lawn, tires, engine, and his *Odyssey* Seminar students, he spent uncountable hours developing a database for the study, which he converted from an older database that a colleague John Mix and he had designed and used to deconstruct and sort every miniscule moment of Homer's epics to find some new insight about the elusive poet. It was more Mix's work than his own. His colleague had a genius for sorting information. He had understood far more than Langley about the ancient dialect shifts in Homeric Greek, and he knew far more than Langley about all the old theories of multiple sources in the *Iliad*. But Mix had failed to get tenure the year before, and since then the database had fallen into disuse like a toolbox left out in the rain. Now it had new life. Full of American country yarners.

* * *

In the terrible days after Carol left to spend Christmas with her mother in Cleveland, taking their two girls, Langley spent all his waking hours on the database, tormented by the image of Carol and the girls sitting in her car in the driveway, not moving, as if waiting for him to come out of the house and stop her, to reach into the car and remove the keys. Or, get into the car himself. Then the image of Carol finally backing out. Sick of stories, sick of trains, sick of ghosts. Needing a rest.

One night when he came home, he was jolted by the sensation of being alone there. Almost as if he was returning from a long and confusing trip to find that Carol, and his children—unlike Penelope and Telemachus—had given up on him and gone away, leaving their dirty dishes in the sink, the garbage overflowing.

On Christmas Eve, Langley was the only one in Hawley-Baines Hall, tinkering with his data, wearing gloves with the tips of the fingers cut off because the heat was turned down to 48. He compared and cross-referenced every imaginable detail of the ghost stories: the make of a disappearing car, and its license number (people usually remembered those things); the time of day when the events allegedly occurred (usually at dusk); how the Jesus-hitchhiker was dressed; if he'd had noticeable body odor; the stories' geographic regions. Also the ages, religious affiliations and education levels of the sources. (This had been the hardest information to gather. People usually clammed up when he asked how much schooling they'd had, and they were visibly offended when he probed their faith.) People could usually pinpoint the date the incidents occurred, because it was almost always near the time that a tragedy had struck their family, almost always a death—sometimes expected, other times not. In fact, the only story that didn't match this was his own family's, Uncle Albert and the ghost train. At least, so far as he knew, there hadn't been a death in his family at that time.

In fact, those tragic memory aids about deaths turned out to be the only real common thread that Langley reaped from this exhaustive study (which, in fact, did exhaust him), months of dogged work to find that the only thing he could draw from it depressed him with its ring of simplistic hocus-pocus.

This realization came to Langley in a bolt, and he stopped typing, and for minutes he could hardly move, as if he'd had a stroke. Recorded Christmas music played from the tower of the campus chapel: *Children go where I send thee! How shall I send thee?* He shut down the computer, locked his office, and walked down the frigid stairs and out into the blowing snow.

* * *

The train through the Andes was sadistically slow. It ground to a halt for unaccountable reasons, and sat sometimes for hours; it was cold at night, and hot in the day. Langley knew better than to drink the water, and instead he stuck to the beer sold to him by people who climbed onto the train when it stopped. And so he was often tipsy. His Spanish was terrible, however, and once he nearly bought a goat by mistake. He was having a frustrating trip.

When he met an Englishman on the train, a well-known travel writer named Terry Spitt, he was overjoyed to meet another English speaker. Spitt's head was bandaged up, and his hair was shaved on the left side. "Frankly," he said, "I have a small hole in my head." And he described a skirmish that he'd wandered into a hundred miles ago, and the unsanitary little hospital he'd lain in for a week. "Rebels, you know. That's why there are all these soldiers on the train. Although, to be sure, I don't know which side to be most afraid of." Indeed, soldiers in the seats across the aisle eyed them with a mixture of hostility and wariness. But Langley knew they were unlikely to be bothered by them.

He breathed deeply and relaxed now, pulling a magnum of wine out of his bag that he had been saving, and shared it with Spitt, pouring it into plastic camp-gear cups, and soon both were very tipsy from drinking at such a high altitude. The ghost-story project was still on his mind—how useless it all seemed to him—although, now that he was far away from it, he could think about it with humor. He told Spitt about it, the whole thing, which had so bitterly frustrated him that he had taken this sudden trip.

But Spitt, who had been slumped tiredly in his seat, suddenly sat up straight. He told Langley that his findings, far from being of no consequence, were fascinating. "Of course, he said, you now have to figure out what it means, that it is all connected to death. That is your next step."

"But," Langley countered, suppressing a burp, "it's something that any reasonably insightful person with a background in psychology could have predicted before I even bothered with the database."

"How so?"

"Well," Langley poured each of them another cup of wine, "they'd conclude—or they ought to—that when there is something like a death in the family, people are grief-stricken; they become delusional."

Spitt shook his head. "I'm afraid that never occurred to me. I had quite a different idea. It sounds to me as if, when death occurs, the veil between the surface world we live in and other-dimensional worlds, becomes rather thin. Do you understand what I mean?"

"Phew!" Langley slapped his leg. "There's an idea to ponder."

Spitt shrugged. "Well, I'm sure you have pondered it, whether or not you'll admit it. I really can't imagine you going to all that work if you had decided, apriori, that there was nothing to any of those accounts of ghosts."

"Ha! Well, it'll be a good thing I have tenure if I ever do suggest such a thing." But, he added, there was one story that fell outside the similarities of all the others, the story of his own uncle. Not only was it the only story about a train, but no one in his family had died around that time. So far as he knew.

Spitt studied him a little humorously. "So far as you know! Well, John, it sounds like there's a small hole in your research. You'd better find that out." Then he chuckled, "Although, listen to me—I'm the one with a bloody hole in my head."

Langley leaned back in his seat with a laugh. "I don't know who I could ask now, anyway. They're all dead." He said the word *dead* the way he might spit out a small stone, as if the whole lot of them in his family had betrayed him by getting old and dying, one by one, much as Carol had betrayed him by running off with his children for Christmas—the continuation of a hex.

"Really! All dead?" asked Spitt.

"My mother's still alive."

"Call her up."

"I suppose I'll have to when I get back," Langley said dismissively.

"Call her up right now."

Langley laughed. "For one thing, my cell won't work up here in the mountains. For another thing, she's not—"

Spitt reached into his jacket and handed Langley a satellite phone. "There. Now, call your dear old mum." When Langley hesitated, he added, "Come, come. You've carried me this far. Let's settle this mystery. Let's tie a nice bow in the end of it."

Langley stared at the phone in his hand. "But, as I was about to say, my mother is an old woman. She's not all there anymore—in her head, I mean."

"You mean she's forgetful?"

"I'm afraid it's worse than that."

"Elderly peoples' long term memory tends to be fairly sharp. Go on, call."

Reluctantly, Langley dialed South Ashburnham, Massachusetts, all the way from the Andes. For God's sake! This was absurd, but Spitt was being so insistent. The voice that answered was the housekeeper's, the Puerto Rican woman Langley paid to take care of his mother, clean house and cook meals. He told her he was calling long distance and wanted to speak to his mother.

When his mother's voice came on, he said hello and asked her if she could hear him.

"Yes, who is this?"

"Mom, this is John."

With a side look at Spitt, he asked her if she remembered the story that Albert, his great uncle, had told about the train that he had nearly collided with, and which had backed away in the dark and disappeared.

"What?...what do you want to know about Albert?"

"I want to know if you remember the story—"

"Albert is dead," she said.

"I know—"

"Albert has been dead for years."

Langley covered the phone with his hand, and said to Spitt, "I don't think this is one of her sharper days." Then he spoke into the phone, "But Mom, do you remember a story that he used to tell about a train?"

"A train? Albert didn't have anything to do with trains. You're thinking of Uncle Emil."

"No, mother," he said in exasperation. And he told her the same story that people in his family had told a hundred times, a hundred different evenings over coffee and Danish pastries. The story that everyone in the family knew by rote. But before he could finish, he could hear his mother trying to interject.

"Who did you say this is?" she asked.

Langley sighed. "Mother, this is John."

"John is dead," she told him.

"No, Mom, this is John, your son. And I'm asking—"

But she insisted. Her son John was dead, and had been dead for....He could hear her call to her housekeeper, and ask her how long her son John had been dead, and he could hear the housekeeper playing along wearily: I doan know, Mizzez. Langley.

The next time the train stopped, Spitt hung his head out of the window, and said they might be at a town. He suggested he get off and see if he could buy another bottle of wine and some bread. Langley nodded, and looked disconsolately out the window at the fog surrounding. They were up in the damned clouds now. He felt drunk, ragged in spirit, and he nodded to sleep. But soon his friend came back and shook him awake.

"You're going to love this," Spitt chucked. "We're not at a station at all. Nor a town or anything else. We've met another train on the track, and both trains refuse to move."

"Really!" Langley said, rubbing his eyes. "What'll we do?"

"We'll do nothing, of course," said the writer. "We're only along for the ride."

Then the train began jolting and jerking, and slowly backing up.

"What? What's going on?" shouted Langley. As Spitt tried to calm him, and as soldiers shot irritable looks at him, he broke away and dashed forward, up two, three cars, knocking people down, hollering, "Stop!"

When a conductor blocked his way, he climbed over two passengers to their open window, and squeezed out, even as the conductor grabbed his coat. Langley dropped to the ground, and rolled over and over on the crushed stones and into the brush. Pulling himself to his feet, he dashed toward the other train.

Rebel insurgents were jumping off the other train and taking up positions on the track. Langley was running toward them as fast as his body would go. He heard gunshots but he didn't know if they were firing at him or over his head. Soldiers who were streaming from Langley's train returned fire, and Langley felt himself hurled forward onto his face where he stared dumbly into the stones. Wine came up his throat, mixed with blood, but he tasted nothing.

Outnumbered, the soldiers backed off after their first volley. But they dragged the crazy, bleeding U. S. professor back to the train. And with soldiers walking beside with their guns at the ready, the train began again, backing slowly into the mountain forest.

Dr. Kershaw's Opinion

THE MOMENT I looked out my office window and saw fifteen or more men coming up the street and turning in at my gate, with Tommy Dubit hobbling in their midst, I suspected what their visit was going to be about: Mr. Dubit had been at the pool hall again, bragging about his wounds. I could see the men's faces flushed from drink, and I was tempted to lock my door. But a doctor cannot lock his door when people are trying to see him.

Mr. Dubit's bullet wounds had become a legend of a kind that idle men seem to find inspiring. He had joined the Army of Northern Virginia decades ago after being disappointed in love, which in itself is an agonizingly ordinary tale. But after Bull Run, Antietam, Gettysburg, and dozens of other fights, he claimed a world record of wounds in the body of a single surviving man. And, he further swore, he was counting only those wounds in which the bullets were still lodged in his body, and they numbered forty. So he claimed. Few believed him, least of all me. My opinion as a physician was that no one can sustain such trauma and go on to live as many years as Mr.

Dubit. But he was forever dropping his trousers in bars to show his less public scars—and proving nothing.

The men crowded into my office, gassy with booze, upsetting a chair. One began to explain, but I raised a hand. "Gentlemen," I said. "I already know what this is about, and you may as well be on your way."

"But Doc," blurted one, "we got twenty bucks riding on this. Can't you x-ray this old boy?"

"I do not operate a betting office," I said.

"We'll pay your going rate plus a handsome tip," another said.

I began to waver. You see, I owned the first and only x-ray equipment in the seven-county region, and I was deeply in debt and anxious to do business to pay for it. So I agreed. It was a difficult examination, with men getting in my way while I forced Mr. Dubit into multiple poses. At last I made them all wait in my parlor while I processed the film, assuring the drunkest of them that there was no technical way that I could alter the images to favor anyone.

Well, the surprise was mine. When I finally pinned up the images—with men's boozy breath over my shoulder—I found seven bullets, and three minnie balls lodged in his central and lower ribs, twelve more of a similar assortment in his right hip, pelvis, and right and left femur, three more in his left clavicle, one in his right humerus, three in the muscle of his left gluteus maximus, one behind his right patella, one in the trapezius muscle of the neck, three lodged around his stomach, one in the sacrospinalis, and two that resembled moons orbiting his liver. Most frightening of all were two projectiles that appeared to be resting in the nest of arteries atop his heart like a couple of birds, another behind a rather ugly facial scar in the area of the palatine bone, and one fragment of a bullet lodged at the base of his skull dangerously near the brain stem.

I said, "I believe that makes forty-one, not forty."

In the ensuing commotion I was forced to re-count three times. And the upshot of it was that, since the number was forty-one, not forty as some had bet, and not fewer as others had wagered, all bets were off.

"Now, Mr. Dubit," I remarked as soon as the squabble died down, "I truly cannot imagine how you can walk, much less work. You're a house painter, are you not? (Though I knew he made his best income at billiards.) I advised him that any exertion might cause one of the fragments near his heart or brain to move a fraction of an inch and kill him, and therefore he belonged in bed. I explained further that, while surgery could remove the most painful bullets in his extremities, those probing his heart and brain were too risky to operate.

"Well, Doc, now you know why a fella drinks,"he answered in the third person, as if his wounds were commonplace. And with that, he got up and lurched out of my office with his bumbling friends behind him.

So, thirty-five years after his last war wound, Tommy Dubit was finally a town hero—until a month later when an elderly woman fired a pistol at him, point blank, in the dark hallway of her home, the entire circumstances of which may never be fully explained, although the district attorney accepted her statement that Mr. Dubit had forced himself upon her person, and that the homicide was therefore justified. In the autopsy I found that this new bullet had entered his body like a cue ball, striking older dormant minnie balls, causing them to ricochet off his ribs, caroming into his heart and lungs. The game was over.

Or at least it was over for Tommy. I have taken up billiards. In fact, since no one ever paid the bill for the x-rays, Mr. Dubit willed me his cue. In the swinging light above the table, the men grin when I bend to shoot. Their bodies are all broken up too. I am just beginning to learn their stories.

The Grand Hotel

RITA HAD A black tomcat with a white head that reminded me of a cat in a tuxedo, particularly the way he'd greet me at her door like Dr. Otternschlag in the 1930s movie *The Grand Hotel*, who stands in the lobby in Berlin and says, "The Grand Hotel. People come, people go. Nothing ever happens." This cat always looked like he was about to recite that speech, even the couple times when Rita and I stumbled in the door drunk together and I was seeing two cats. But the animal was right—to extend the analogy—things were in kind of a freeze between Rita and myself. Nothing was happening.

Her apartment was on a little street off Waverley in Greenwich Village. Something about the position of the street made it act like a wind tunnel. Rita always left her kitchen window open so that Lewis—the cat's name—could climb out onto the fire escape if he wanted to, and so her kitchen was also windy. The wind would blow the salad right out of your bowl.

"Can't we close the window?" I asked once.

"No," she answered. "Going out there is the only

fun Lewis gets."

I was teaching in Syracuse then. To see Rita on weekends, I'd drive to Tarrytown and take the train into the city. But one night we had a big fight—I don't remember what it was about, I only remember that we were yelling—and I left her apartment so stunned that I was already on the train heading up the river before I started to sob, and sobbed so hard that I got off in the wrong town at two in the morning. Everything was closed, and finally I slept in a clump of bushes. Imagine: one of the country's foremost scholars of modern European history sleeping in somebody's hedge.

But, the next day it dawned on me that I'd left her apartment without my overnight bag, so I took the Metro back down to the city and pounded on her door. She opened a crack with the chain still hooked and looked me up and down. She said, "So where is he?"

I said, "Where's who?"

Several minutes of ballyhoo went on before I realized she was accusing me of taking her cat the night before, because Lewis was gone, vanished. We looked out her kitchen window and saw huge falcons circling above the roof, and it happened that a siren was going off on the street at the time, and it gave me a chill like a little air raid. Raptors must have snatched him up!

We scrambled up the stairs to the roof, afraid of what we'd find, but saw nothing, no fur, no blood, no collar with a little bell. She talked me into getting a running start and jumping the alley to the next roof to look farther. I could hardly believe the stupidity of what I was doing; even as I leapt I thought of Lewis saying, "People come, people go." *The Grand Hotel* was also the movie where Greta Garbo spoke her famous line, "I want to be alone." Which of course is impossible: no one can be alone. I barely cleared the parapet, and rolled onto the roof—easily the most dangerous thing I've ever done in my life. Imagine: Professor Falls Four Stories to His Stupid Death, covered with a blanket on the sidewalk like a wino. Anyway, there was nothing to see on that other roof but more tar paper.

My ankle was twisted now, so I definitely wasn't jumping back. But, when I started down the stairs of that other building, I ran into a big Doberman in the hall, drooling at me in the dark. So, I was stuck on the roof for hours while Rita telephoned about fifty people in the other building—starting with the one person she knew there, and getting referred to another and another— before she found the woman who owned the monster. Sachel was its name. The woman, clad in a ratty housecoat and two shaggy Heathcliff slippers, opened the door to the roof and said to me, "C'mon, you big baby, the dog isn't going to hurt you."

Rita and I were silent over dinner in a bar on Mac-Dougall. I think she'd given up on Lewis being my fault. But every time it seemed like we were about to really talk, one of us would order more drinks. Finally we went back to her apartment, with me limping painfully, and fell into bed like a pair of trees and snored.

I dreamed I was jumping from roof to roof all over the West Village. My pockets were full of diamonds, some of which fell out every time I leapt, glittering in the streetlights like shattered glass. I wondered, were they my diamonds or Rita's?

But we woke at almost the same moment—after midnight—with the same realization: that when we'd come in the door, Lewis had greeted us as always, and we hadn't even noticed because we were both drunk and distraught. Rita hollered, "Lewis!" We both jumped out of bed and found him sitting on the table like one of the New York Public Library lions. Rita petted him for hours.

My theory was that he'd jumped from the fire escape into another apartment. Maybe the people there knew *The Grand Hotel,* and Lewis reminded them of Dr. Otternschlag, and they were waiting for him to speak. Or maybe the new people reminded Lewis of us, like two people playing us in a movie. Only different—everything different, but the same. And, just as with us, nothing ever happened.

Children of the Trees

IN MY LATE teens I started driving into the city to a small movie house that showed foreign films. Bergman, Truffaut, Fellini, and so on. This was in the Midwest where I grew up. No one else in my little farm town was interested in those films that had so hooked me, that were at once exotic, intellectual, and erotic, and I always went to the city alone.

The theater was in a border neighborhood, in the northside of which were chic shops and cafes, while to the south was a skid-row of winos, junkies, and gangs. The owner was a joking fat man with a pallid complexion, who always wore a black suit so that when he walked down the dark aisle he became a floating head blooming upon a white collar. After a few weekends he began to notice me, and we finally introduced ourselves. I can't remember his name now; but whenever I came in after that he'd joke, "The farm contingent is here!"

One movie I saw there has stayed with me unlike any other. It was called *Children of the Trees* —low-budget, black and white, unknown actors. A group of medieval European boys murder their feudal landlord's over-seer with shovels and picks, and then flee into the woods to establish some sort of children's Utopia, although they have no such words for it and only a half-baked plan to begin with. In the woods they create absurd masks of bark, thinking that they can actually hide their identities.

One night when I came into the theater, the owner had to rush to his office to take an urgent phone call, and he nervously asked me to stand in for him for a few minutes and take tickets. On several more nights he asked me to do that—he seemed always in a dire sprint to the phone. While standing in for him got me into the theatre free, I missed the beginning of films, which irked me. I also had the uneasy feeling that he really didn't have to take a call, that he was in some kind of trouble and didn't want to be seen in the lobby.

After they establish a camp in the woods, the boys discover, to their dismay, that they have to defend them-selves constantly—not against the nobleman's forces, as it turns out, but against their own families, serfs who come after them with pitchforks and the like, because by murdering the overseer the boys have upset the benign neglect of the lord, bringing hellish punishments on the whole population. The strongest boy, the one who had ac-tually instigated the murder, tries to rally other the boys to fight, to keep their masks on. But their lives have be-come a nightmare.

Probably owing to its low budget, some dialogue was untranslated; or the subtitles were monosyllabic—"Quick! Run! To the trees!"—when the actors seem to be saying much more. But it was so well acted that I could have understood it perfectly with no dialogue.

You might expect that other films of that period, like Bergman's *Hour of the Wolf,* or Antonioni's *Blow Up*, would have stayed with me all these years, and they have to a degree. But it is this simple film by a director whose name I can't remember which comes back to me when I think of those years when I drove so far to see foreign movies. I have never seen that film again.

Much later—twenty years or so—I was divorced and living alone in the city. I became one of those men standing in the laundromat at midnight, watching my clothes go around and around. I had tried to cheer myself by buying all new clothes, but they still had to be washed and dried. And so, there I would be, leaning against a table in a meditation of tumbling shirts or reading discarded magazines.

One midnight I saw a man standing nearby in a black Navy P-coat, his hair tussled, and a stubble on his face that edged nearly to his eyes. Someone was worse off than me, although that knowledge was not especially comforting. But I thought I recognized him, and when he finally saw me staring he glared at me, and I felt obliged to speak.

"If I'm not mistaken," I started, searching my memory's pockets, "you used to run a theatre. You showed—."

"No," he cut me off, shaking his head. "I used to tell people I ran movie theatres, that's all. I didn't really."

"But," I said, "I used to stand in for you when you had all those phone calls."

At this, his eyes widened in what I suspect was recognition. But he said, "No."

Annoyed, I said, "Best movies I ever saw. Do you remember *Children of the—*."

This time he turned and walked away, shaking his head wearily.

So we couldn't be friends again. And that was all right. I was in a state of grief and bitterness, and didn't feel like being chummy anyway. I was uncomfortable in the laundromat with him now, and I took my clothes out of the dryer; put a still-damp shirt on over my tee-shirt, and left.

I thought, maybe one night long ago he had stepped out of his movie house and walked the wrong way, into skid row. But, as I was to learn much later when I read his obituary, loan sharks had taken his theater and beat him up periodically until he'd either managed to disappear from their sight or they'd lost interest in him.

But, about that film: Being chased by serfs, the boys finally have to split up and run their separate ways. And then the movie's focus shifts to the strongest boy, the instigator of the violence, as he zig-zags through the woods. He happens upon a man and a woman making love. After his initial shock he steals the man's clothes, and although he has to roll up the sleeves and trouser legs, he now has a new disguise and he runs out of the woods toward another village where smoke is rising from cook fires in the distance. He is ravenously hungry. As he runs, he stumbles over the trouser cuffs that keep coming unrolled.

On his way, a ragged old man on a horse stops and, drawing his horse sideways to block the boy's path, he asks, "Are you from Ogala?"

Terrified, the boy says, "No, I am not. I only look like I am from Ogala." He says more that goes untranslated. But the gist is, his story is full of holes.

The old man laughs and climbs down from the horse. For a moment the boy thinks the man is going to give him a ride. But then he pulls a rope and irons from his bag. The old man laughs as he walks toward the boy who stumbles on his pants trying to get away and falls on the path.

"Only one world," the old man's dialogue appears across the screen at his feet. "There is nowhere to hide."

Uncle Lucky

IN MY FAMILY, two generations before me, was a Corporal and Mrs. Cortland, retired. As everyone knows, corporal is not a distinguished rank. No one, retired from the army, would go around in polite society calling himself Corporal—except my Uncle Lucky, whose full name was Cpl. Birch Cortland. It brought titters everywhere he and my aunt went. Whenever they were announced some poor butler would stumble and get red in the face, thinking he had gotten someone's title abhorrently wrong. But Uncle Lucky thought it was a great joke, one that brought the rich and unsuspecting dangerously into his sphere.

You've heard of soldiers of fortune. Uncle Lucky was a soldier of luck. He served no other cause than luck.

Once, around 1922 or '23, Cpl. and Mrs. Cortland were traveling and they stopped in Corinth, where he fell in love with a Spanish cigar heiress, named Corizon, who had an Italian husband named Cortese who had an estate in Cortona. The two of them, Uncle Lucky and the heiress, fled to Athens, and boarded the H.M.S. Cortenwald, which ship was blown off course, and docked in Corsica where the corporal and mistress disembarked to do some shopping.

Immacula Corizon-Cortese had been carrying a large sum of cash, both her own and her husband's, which was mysteriously missing from a secret pouch in her corselet an hour after my uncle had escorted her from the boat. He reported the theft to the Corsican police on her behalf. And then disappeared himself.

When police investigated they became confused by the statement of events from the wildly excited heiress. They threw up their hands. She went next to the US Consulate to denounce Uncle Lucky, but the consul was just as confused. He heard: Corporal, Cortland, Cortenwald, Cortese, Corizon, Corinth, Cortona, off-course, corselet, the Corporal's old court-marshal (a past trouble when he'd been busted down from a much higher rank, and which he'd confessed to her aboard the Cortenwald over a bottle of Corbieres), and that the Corsican police had traced the Corporal to Corte, where they lost his trail. The consul threw up his hands.

Uncle Lucky dropped out of sight from time to time over the ensuing years, whenever he needed to. I first met him at my seventh birthday party in our back yard in Buffalo, New York. He was broke, alone, gloomy, and ate most of the food. A few months later he was rich again and living in San Francisco. And my aunt was with him once more. It was later, when I was older, that I realized my aunt wasn't the saint that I'd believed her to be, that she was in fact his confederate in many of his elaborate and complicated flim-flams, including the Corinth affair, where she had played the wronged wife with brilliance.

One doesn't naturally inherit luck, and I didn't inherit Uncle Lucky's. We call people lucky who inherit money, but that is a misnomer. Inheritance is fortune. Luck is hotter, and burns faster, but keeps coming back again if you're a truly lucky person. People who inherit money are often unlucky people. I inherited a little, but I'm naturally unlucky, and I lost it all. When dice are rolled, I lose, usually. And in my one and only foray into crime—I stole a Davy Crockett pencil in the fourth grade—I was caught before I left the school building. I was shamed and officially ostracized, and for two weeks I had to put my head down on my desk during free-period activities. (Not that I still want to steal, mind you. I don't—I don't think.) My bad luck has extended to other areas of my life. When the woman I desired more than any other in the world finally agreed to go to bed with me, I couldn't get an erection. But, in the taxi taking me home from the fiasco, I got a stiffy that almost tore out the front of my pants. The point is, I'm like most people, unlucky more than I'm lucky.

Uncle Lucky was busted down to corporal from colonel shortly before Armistice, 1918, because he stole an army vehicle on a drunken AWOL tour of the French countryside. He avoided the firing squad because he'd taken the daughter of a French major general with him, and the American Army wanted to keep her name diplomatically out of it, and avoid the publicity of an embattled court marshal. So, they quietly busted him, and let it go at that. Yet, somehow he ended up with the girl's money. According to my family, he took the rank-busting with equanimity, if not outright cheerfulness. Much responsibility goes with being a colonel, and he wanted no more of it.

The real history of human knowledge is a disordered encyclopedia, among which is, somewhere, the equation of luck, just as somewhere in an asylum are the keys to the door. Fortune may favor the prepared, but luck is cabbalistic.

A picture of a lucky man and his wife grace the mantle in my living room. When I'm tired and discouraged I look at it. Somewhere in his eyes is the key to this workaday asylum, I think. And I look away. Afraid that I will see it, afraid that I will suddenly understand that I am wrong, that it isn't, after all, luck.

Traber Cripes is Dead. Was Noted Skeptic

TRABER CRIPES, A man famous for doubting "damned near everything," died on May 5, said his assistant, Sam Zingman, himself a leading media skeptic. The cause of death was "complications of congestive heart failure," Mr. Zingman said, adding, "if you take the doctor at his word. Traber Cripes always asserted that most people die of broken hearts, and that the only truly human response to a culture of mass misinformation is heartbreak."

Mr. Cripes was 57, and lived in suburban Rochester, New York, where his assistant operates the Traber Cripes Foundation for Open and Free Information.

In a career colored by law suits and legal injunctions, including numerous restraining and cease-and-desist orders, and even jail time, Mr. Cripes loudly disrupted scientific conferences, media forums such as *Meet the Press*, and even presidential press conferences. He disputed such widely held views as the 92-million-mile distance to the sun, which he baldly asserted is only 17,500 miles from earth. Mr. Cripes apparently made this unorthodox calculation with an ordinary sextant.

He believed, or at least asserted, that most US voting machines are rigged, and always have been. He claimed that cigarettes, while indeed causing lung cancer, also promote mental health, and are therefore worth the risk since it is better to have a happy short life than a miserable long one. Always able to find supporting statistics, Mr. Cripes pointed out that the rise of mental illness cases in the United States corresponds roughly to the decline in per-capita smokers.

He believed that flying saucers are Israeli spy planes. He believed that aurora borealis is created by Eskimos sending signals to the Russians with giant ice-mirrors.

Various reports claim that Mr. Cripes married and divorced only once, while others have him marrying some seventeen times. His foundation would not confirm any report about his marriages.

Mr. Cripes first came to renown in 1959 when, at the age of 10, he claimed that there was only one dog named Lassie who played all parts in all the famous TV episodes, contrary to widely accepted information that there were upward of twelve dog-stand-ins trained to play various tricks. The *Lassie* dispute led to his first arrest when he broke into the famous dog's kennel at a Hollywood studio. He was charged as a juvenal offender on that occasion, and his parents grounded him for six months. Years later, he still claimed he had found only one collie in the pen, but that "studio thugs" had smashed his camera, thus destroying the evidence.

He was an early political advisor to Ronald Reagan, and was believed to be the source of the former president's long-held belief that nuclear ICBMs could be called back to their bases after launching. But Mr. Cripes's well-known assertions that the missiles could be re-called were actually part of his broader theory that liberals and pro-Soviets in the scientific community had kept that fact a secret (even from the Pentagon) in order to prevent the United States from staging simulated nuclear attacks to frighten the USSR and China into submission.

Mr. Cripes became less visible in recent years, leading many media watchers to speculate that he was mellowing, even tiring of his constant public battles. He spent more time at his Rochester foundation and less time stumping and debating.

Yet the familiar, outrageous Traber Cripes burst into the news again last year with a new claim, as cantankerous as any he'd made before. He said that there have been twelve Fidel Castros, not one, as most believe. He even claimed to have met secretly in West Palm Beach with four retired Castros, and that one was actually a bearded woman. These claims prompted the Cuban premier (purportedly the real one) to invite Mr. Cripes to visit him in Havana and to count the freckles on his posterior, the exact number of which, the Castro source asserted, has been on file at the CIA for many years.

That Mr. Cripes did not accept Castro's invitation surprised many media watchers, who saw it as the very sort of comedic event that Mr. Cripes seemed to crave, and led many to suspect that he really was losing his pizzazz. Mr. Zingman, however, said that Mr. Cripes declined to travel to Havana out of respect for President Bush's ban on travel to Cuba.

If that were the case, some media pundits claim, it may indicate that, far from being in decline, Mr. Cripes's star had been once again on the rise, if only behind official Administration curtains.

In the Age of Curiosity

WE DID NOT know the tribe that overran us. Later we would know more than we wanted to know about them, but when they attacked our village and forced us to lie on our backs, they were just hostile strangers. They weighted our hands and feet down with rocks, cut off our clothes and examined our private parts to see if they were like their own. They measured and sniffed us, then pinched and wiggled and tickled us to gauge our reactions. But when the first lightning struck the hill they looked frantically about, jumping and moving their lips in *boggle babboo*, which puzzled us—we knew nothing yet of words. They panicked at the ensuing thunder, stampeded, and by the time the first rain drops hit our faces they were gone. The gods had answered our prayers, although our prayers were only fervent thoughts and grunts, because, as I said, we knew nothing of words or of names.

When we finally freed our limbs from under the rocks, we stormed their village, catching them off guard, and killed them all, save one, a woman whom I tied to a tree. She yelled in my face in *boggle babboo* until I grunted and fluttered my fingers on my lips. Slowly she understood what I wanted, and in the following days and nights of her captivity she taught me to speak. First I learned the names of my body parts. I grunted at my brothers to come to us, and they learned the same words from her. The *wombogs* that dangled between their legs, for example.

"*Wombog,*" she said, grabbing one brother's *wombog.*

He grinned and replied, "*Wombog,*" and put his finger between her legs, and received a vicious kick to his *wombog.*

Slowly, after more kicks and threats, he came to understand what *wombog* meant, and what it did not mean.

Most of our word lessons were less brutal, but even more exciting. Our new knowledge not only pacified us, but blossomed new curiosity. We kept calling to her and pointing to yet another of our body parts, and she would (somewhat more patiently now) give us yet another word. Never had we been so inspired, and we soon began thinking beyond ourselves to the trees and the sky-fires, to the white stone in the night sky, and the river, and she gave us name after name as well as hundreds of words that made bridges between the names.

I brought the woman home and had two wives. My first wife took to the language frighteningly fast as if she'd known it all along, and soon the two were slinging so many names at each other that I became utterly confused and had to leave my house for a time. But all in all, things were improved. My brothers and I took the names she gave us, and we felt as if we'd had them forever but had not known them, and thus had not known ourselves (much less one another). Now it was as if the lightning that had chased our attackers away had also illuminated us, given us a new fire kindled in our mouths, that burned a tallow of words.

But now we began using our words to explain ourselves to ourselves and to one another. And this was troublesome. There were ideas to coax from one another like animals from their holes. Hurts needed to be described, hurts in our body parts mostly, and in our mouths, but also deeper in our breasts. We almost forgot to hunt, since so much time was spent in the new hunting ground of our hearts.

Then one morning, after a long night of talking and arguing, we slept a little longer, and when we opened our eyes, strangers were standing over us. For a moment I thought they were my brothers, as if the new names had given them different faces. But they were not us.

Another curious tribe had come to pin our arms and legs to the ground with rocks. I spoke to them in *boggle babboo*, urging them to cut off our clothes, make their inspections of our *wombogs*, and *fweehs*, and *bluggocurs*, and get it over with, and leave us. But they weren't interested in our body parts. These men wanted to know what was inside our heads, and they started cracking them open one by one.

Rome

SOMETIMES IT TAKES forever to get off a bus. Especially in the winter, when everyone ahead of you is pulling on their coats, buttoning up. Yet it wasn't winter—Van Nord kept reminding himself of that. Not winter. It had been winter when he went into the hospital. Not winter now he was out. Hell of a winter storm when he went in. Blossoms now, and the sun was burning.

"It's a beautiful spring day, Mr. Van Nord," the doctor had said at their last session, just before they drove him to the bus station. "Go on out there and get a new start. You agreed to live with your daughter, isn't that right?"

"Yes," Van Nord had replied.

"And remind me, where does she live?"

"Rome, sir."

"Oh!" the doctor's face lit. "Which one?"

"Rome, New York, sir. Fifty miles up the road."

"Ah well," the doctor had said, tapping his pen on his desk and looking out the window. "But it's hot enough today to be like the real Rome. Don't you think?"

The real Rome. Van Nord had never known but one Rome, the town where he'd always lived and where he'd spent most of his life going house to house reading gas meters. And the old colonial Fort Stanwix just outside of town, where he'd had a little tourist-trap job playing a drunken muleskinner to perfection. A little bar in town where he'd once danced an embracing, mesmerizing waltz with a professional dancer—or so she'd said she was. They'd danced to "Help Me Make It through the Night." For years after that beautiful evening he'd continued dropping endless quarters into the juke machine, playing the same song, a little heart-shaped stain on the song's title card, right next to the selection number: D4. He'd driven people nuts with that song.

When he was too full of whiskey to walk to the machine himself, he'd give a handful of quarters to some chippy and tell her, "Play D4, as many times as it'll let you." He had to hear that song. Otherwise he couldn't get through the night. Couldn't sleep. Even in the hospital he dreamed D4, and even went through the motion of dropping a quarter because it made him hear the opening notes: *Take the ribbon from your hair.* "D4," he'd whisper to himself whenever they wheeled him into the room where they fastened the electrodes to his head. A mantra, D4, D4, D4. Until they put the rubber puck in his mouth, and even then he'd chant, D4, D4 through his nose.

One stormy winter day the Indians had suddenly attacked old Fort Stanwix, and the captain had told him to forget the muleskinner act and help man the battlements. The main gate swung shut, and the tourists who happened to be in the fort at the moment were led to the main cabin for shelter. Muskets roared as he climbed the ladder to the ramparts, snow swirling, almost blinding him. Flaming arrows sailed overhead. Iroquois kept coming and coming, wave after wave, they didn't seem to care how many of them died. Cannon fire shook the fort to its foundations.

But then, when he looked behind and down at the main yard, he saw that dancing girl from years before. She was walking with her purse strap over her shoulder, a cigarette in her lips, and getting her car keys out of her coat pocket like nothing was going on. What the hell was she doing in here?

He skinned his leg badly climbing back down the ladder. But he caught up with her, and hysterically she beat him away. He growled, "Get back in the cabin." He warned her that it was she the Indians were after. But she ignored him and strode away, slinging a curse at him over her shoulder. Finally, he jumped on her and wrestled her to the snowy ground.

The next thing he remembered, he was in irons lying on his back, a bad lump on his head. As near as he could tell the Indians had been beaten while he was unconscious, since all he saw now were state police standing around, snow on their big hats. No Indians. Some day history might exonerate him. But not soon.

Spring, Van Nord reminded himself now. It was spring now in Rome. He climbed off the bus, and began walking up Main Street. A cafe' had moved its tables out on the walk and people were sitting in the sun drinking and eating. But he saw no one that he knew, and that was a relief. He had been away a long time.

He bought a pint and sat on his suitcase to drink it. He had to make a decision. It was a mile to his daughter's house, and she didn't know he was coming. Across the street was the little bar with D4 on the box, but that way was also dangerous, people who hated him, people who never wanted to hear that song again as long as they lived. Actually, people all over town hated him: the loony man who snuck around people's houses reading their gas meters and writing in his little notebook. He was even accused of looking in windows.

But there was also Fort Stanwix. Yes, the boys at the fort, the ones who'd survived the attack—they would be glad to see him. They would sit around the fire with him and tell stories of the attack. He finished his pint, and pitched it into an alley. He started walking toward the fort. Darkness was coming down. Maybe they'd be roasting a goose. Maybe they would be drinking pints. Maybe he should buy another one just in case.

Along the road he stopped and took a sweater out of his suitcase, his stocking cap and coat, and put them on, buttoning the coat up to his throat. For it had begun to snow.

Part III:

Wild

Book Review

A Pig in Paris: Stories by Steven Huff. Rochester, New York, Big Pencil Press, 158 pp.

THIS BOOK GOT off to a poky start: I had to put it down a dozen times to let the dog out or back in, and I kept losing my place. Then a friend wanted to go to a movie, so I went along. When I got back the book was lost, later emerging from under the bed with the dust mop. Tried to get the hang of it later by carrying it to lunch, but somebody's newspaper was left on the counter with the story of a triple murder (and I'm such a sucker for murders), which stole my attention. A few hours later, when I realized I'd left the book there, I called the diner, and that was when the twist-noir finally occurred.

The waitress who answered the phone (in a voice like she was blowing smoke through her nose) said, "I'm reading it on my break, and you can have it when I'm done. Not until."

So, I waited in unbearable suspense—because I'd had a girlfriend once who chain-smoked Luckies, even during sex, and she'd had a voice much like this waitress. She would have one roaring climax after another like a train that keeps rolling by when you're sitting anxiously at the crossing, and I couldn't help but envision her on the other end of the phone. So, frankly, this waitress' voice woke up my rooster—and I finally got in my car and drove there. I mean, what the hell.

That's how we met. Her name was Dearie, and she actually looked tougher than her voice sounded. She was married to a milquetoast named Jonathan, but our storm of love got started anyway. One night we made our escape together in her station wagon on a road that curled up the night like ivy. We carried with us everything we valued or were afraid to leave (her daughter in the first place, the *Pig in Paris* book in the second—although by now I didn't know when I was ever going to read it). We had a fistful of bad checks we planned to pass as soon as we came to a town with a name stupid enough that we could assume they'd accept them.

But there's always a rearview mirror in a story like this, plus headlights that wouldn't quit bearing down on us from behind. Of course, you know who was tailing us: her husband—the predictable, soft-spoken, sulking Jonathan. His last name was Johnson. I'm not kidding. So, he was Jonathan "Yes-Dearie" Johnson. If you put that in a book nobody would believe it. But there he was riding our asses, doing eighty, laying on the horn. I figured he'd finally blown his gourd. So, to calm my nerves, I tried to read another few pages of *A Pig in Paris* by flashlight. But, rattled as hell, with Dearie's hand on my leg, her kid yelling, her husband's high beams on the back of my head, and a pocketful of his checks, I didn't get very far.

I knew a big climax was coming, and it came—we hit a moose (Did I mention this was New Hampshire?). Jonathan, following too close like an idiot, piled into our ass-end so hard his false teeth ended up on our dashboard. Jesus, what a scene: steam, glass, moose-meat, kid crying her eyes out, husband crawling around in the road looking for his teeth and his glasses. In the hospital I sat on a bench while Dearie was in the ER with her husband, and I read the book to the kid for something to do. I think she liked it, to tell you the truth.

Enough

AL. HE WAS tired, more than he'd ever been before. Yet, for the past five nights, every time he closed his eyes his worries lit up the inside of his skull like a bare light bulb, until he wondered, if he died would his head keep right on worrying? Al was a veteran worrier, but his main problem this month was the constant rain that wouldn't let him into his fields to plant, rain that whipped his roof, his cows sinking in mud up to their udders. Now, after so much sleeplessness, he was walking in new territory where things looked askew, where people had begun to look vague and insubstantial. He'd begun to see shadows in the barn that moved about and seemed to be watching him.

When his alarm rang this morning, he'd sat up in the dark on the bedside, pulled on his coveralls and Carhart coat, and tromped unslept down the stairs, pulled on his boots in the mudroom, and walked out to the tractor shed. He didn't stir Lena to say good morning—Lena, who two nights in a row had fumed about having had enough of it all. "I've had a *'nuff...'nuff...'nuff!*" she'd barked last night. He was sure she'd be gone this morning before he came in for breakfast. Gone like a dollar bill left on a bar.

However, he felt sorry. For Lena. Yes, the God's-honest truth, he couldn't blame her. She had her shadows too.

But young Johnny. He was about as good as rain. Home from Skidmore College where he'd taken up dreaming. Metal hanging all over his face. Yesterday Al came upon him in the milking parlor hooking up a cow to the milker, and the boy seemed asleep with his face mushed against her belly. Al asked his son, "You hear anything in there?" And when Johnny looked at him vacantly, he'd added another question, "You milkin' or dreamin'?"

And Johnny had given him a sage answer, "'In dreams begin responsibility'." But Al was too tired to think about what was rolled up in that statement.

The morning was frigid, but at least the rain had stopped. He buttoned his coat, hitched the plow, and climbed onto the John Deere, muttering, "Had a *'nuff... nuff.*" As he steered into the north field, rodents leapt about in his headlights like little clowns. Other shapes leapt about too, but they were only shadows.

They were only shadows, but they climbed aboard Al's tractor, and took the wheel from his hands. Reached warmly around him. The shadows did. And turned the tractor toward the lane and the far fields.

Drivers on their way to work at the crack of dawn screeched to a halt as a tractor dragged a plow banging across the road. They watched it bull ahead, cutting one long stripe over a rain-soaked hill—a man slumped over the machine's steering wheel. It plowed across somebody's front yard, took down some clotheslines, a Virgin statue, splashed through a retention pond, banged across a service road, and cut a strip in the infield at the Jefferson Middle School.

But, in his dream, Al was already onto the interstate throttling toward Washington, plowing toward the White House. Ha, now he was chasing the president himself down a long beach, yelling, "Giddy-up," laughing like he'd never done before. "Had a 'nuff, yet?" he hollered, bearing down on the chief of all chiefs, when he suddenly felt tired again, even in his dream, and he stopped the machine in its tracks. "What's the president got to do with anything?" he asked out loud, and climbed down from the tractor. Al kicked some sand at nothing. He kicked more sand at more nothing.

Lena had oatmeal bubbling on the stove, and sausage frying. She hadn't left. But neither was she in a good mood. She looked at Johnny hanging over his coffee, sniffing through his nose ring. "Go flag your father to come in for breakfast," she said, and added with more force, "Now!"

Slowly Johnny got up and pulled on his parka, and walked out onto the north field, sod squishing under his feet. But what he saw in the field befuddled him. Over the slope a single plow path veered away from the regular field pattern and headed down a slope, busted through a fence and wandered crookedly beyond the trees. "Oh, my God," Johnny said. He started to follow the long, crazy furrow, then he stopped and looked back at the house as if considering: should he go or turn back?

Johnny decided to go, and began to run. But when he started he didn't know how far he would go. Or how far was enough. Or how far.

Hard Luck

Hey, come here, Johnny! Have a seat before you fall down, and let me buy you a cup of coffee. Don't worry, I ain't gonna play Pollyanna, try to kid you that you look good after losing your house. The fact is, Johnny, you look awful. It's too late to warn you not to borrow from banks. But I will say one thing: sooner or later things've gotta get better for you. Believe me when I tell you.

When this kind of thing happens—I mean like happened to you—it just goes to show: the cops are leaning on the wrong guys in this country. I mean, look at the so-called mob. Okay, so they lend you money and you can't pay them back. What do they do? They send a guy over to break your leg. Then you sit around for six months doing crossword puzzles, taking it easy while you heal up. After that, you start over with a clean bill. But the last thing they'd ever do is turn your family out of your house.

But these damn banks—I don't have to tell you.

I borrowed some mob money one time, right from Salvatore himself. Told him I wanted to buy out Sammy's grocery store, and that was the truth. But, I was a stupid kid. That cash wasn't in my pocket ten minutes before I was heading for the race track. I was gonna double the money, pay Salvatore back, and have the store free and clear. Right? I lost the whole bundle inside of two hours. I was scared then, and I didn't know where the hell to run.

But, about the same time Salvatore's daughter Marie runs off with one of the grooms from the stable over at the track. What the hell makes a good girl do a crazy thing like that? 'Cause that guy didn't have two nickels to cover his eyeballs whenever they caught up with him. Well, Salvatore didn't know who to go after first—me or that hairy ape of a groom. Finally, he did the only thing a father could do. He put out an all-points on Marie, and a contract on the horse groomer.

Well, it just so happened Marie and the groom split for New Jersey. Salvatore's buddy Falletti saw them leaving a roadhouse just outside of Atlantic City, but he lost their trail. The damned groom must have been driving a hundred miles an hour. But I got friends down there in Jersey. So, some accommodations got made—you know what I mean?—'cause they'd already heard about the stupid thing I did up here and the trouble I was in. So the deal they made was, they'd go find Marie and the groom if Salvatore went easy on me.

A week goes by while Salvatore's getting things tucked away down there in Jersey, my friends closing in on the groom and Marie. Meanwhile I'm going nuts from the silence, 'cause I don't even know there's been this deal made. Right? When Salvatore finally sends Paul and Frankie over to see me, I'm sweating .38 slugs, thinkin' they're gonna bust both my legs and my neck too. Paul and Frankie just stood there in my living room looking at me till I busted up crying like baby with the croup.

And you know what they finally done? They whacked me upside the head a couple times, and they picked me up by the belt and gave me the biggest snuggy I ever got in my life. Then they bent my pinkie finger back till it snapped.

Few days later, Salvatore sends word he wants me to come and see him. I go into his house shaking like a wet mutt. He goes, Tommy! I go, Yeah, Godfather. He goes, How's your finger? I go, It's gonna be okay, Godfather, thanks for askin'. He goes, You learn your lesson? I go, Sure, Godfather.

Then he hands me the deed to the store. He goes, I ever hear of you goin' to the track again, I'm gonna bust both your legs and all your fingers. Believe me when I tell you. I go, Why you doin' this for me, Godfather?

'Cause, he goes, if it wasn't for the deal we had to make 'cause of you, we never would of found Marie and that ugly groom. Now she's home safe and sound. God's been good to both of us, Tommy. So I'm doing what God wants me to do. *Capisci*?

I did okay in that little store. I mean, I'm not rich or nothing. In fact, I had some hard times. It ain't been all roses and petunias. I wish I could help you out now with those damn banks foreclosing on you. I could get Salvatore to help you if he wasn't in the slammer now himself. But you come over to the store this afternoon and I'll load you up with some groceries. Your credit's good with me, Johnny.

What? You want to know what happened to that two-bit groom? Drink your coffee, Johnny.

Wild

YOU KNOW ABOUT the clown who drinks. We don't mean the nit wits you meet at some party. But the clown, the real one, who drinks. He's the only professional clown working in your town, the only one with a block ad in the Yellow Pages. CLOWN it reads, with a phone number that rings an answering machine somewhere. His other ad in a local tabloid reads WILL CLOWN, which, compared to the Yellow Pages ad, sounds contradictory. Is he a verb or a noun? Will he or is he? But, of course, if he were not already a clown, he would never have the courage to take out such an ad.

But, we've asserted that he drinks. We haven't established that he does, only asserted, but for a good reason as we'll see. Because of his ad, though, we know that he exists—if we accept that what is so apparent *is*.

Although you haven't yet thought of him overly much, sooner or later your curiosity will grab the wheel and you'll go looking for him. Calling him would be too direct. One day you'll flip through the Yellow Pages under C for COLD STORAGE, and CLOWN will come up, glaring at you. Or while looking for CARTING, or COBALT, or CORN, there'll be CLOWN once more, surprising you like turning over cards you thought were kings of spades or tens of diamonds, but finding the joker instead. Wild, in other words.

How does a man—you assume the clown is male—find enough clowning business in a little town like yours? How does he manage his psyche, being the only one? Where does he worship, where does he buy his underwear? Does a woman love him, and has she born him children who go to school with your kids, and fight them on the playground? When driving does he cut down your street past your house on his way to clowning jobs? Do you even know him and don't realize he is the clown?

In other words—and this is the real question we're leading to—what does he find among us that is so funny? A clown is only funny if he acts out what he knows of us, and shows us how funny we are. Are we funny because we're merely odd, or because we're disturbing?

Now, why do we assume he drinks? Well, taken all together, because of his anonymity, lack of peers, his probable use of multiple masks, he must drink for relief. The preponderance of people laughing at him. And the fact that he is probably, truth be told, a failure. Yes, he is a failure. Why else would he be still working in your little town? If he were better than a merely good clown, he would have gone to Las Vegas or Atlantic City. And if he were a great clown, he'd be on TV. Or even if he is great, but didn't move to one of those centers of the entertainment industry because he hadn't the courage, then he is a failure for that reason. So, you have to assume he's throwing down a few shots at every party where he's hired to clown, telling himself he's not up to snuff.

But what if it's not about failure, what if it's because of us? Maybe—and here we go back to the substance of our real question—we provide such a trove of comic material by being ourselves that he loves us and can't leave us. Such love drives people to drink, too, you know.

Is it the way we talk, eat, breath? Our clothes? Our—God forbid!—odor?

You'll start looking for him in the better bars where everyone who is anyone drinks. Then you'll move on to the nameless bars, where you'll see no one who looks even flamboyant (we shun flamboyance here, anyway), much less a man with a red-knob nose and orange hair. You'll have a drink here, another there. Until you are drunk yourself, and making people laugh at you.

You may find him, finally, in the chewed end of your nervous cigar. In the lava of your smoke, or refracted in the ennui of bar mirrors, in the worm that dances whenever you pour the bottle. In the promenade of upstairs window-lights, like the rooms of the moon, as you stumble on your peregrinations in search of the clown. In the small stars that form of oxygen mixed when scared lovers talk tricks. In the high lights, or low. Somewhere, God yes, some clown who thinks nobody knows him.

But you'll find him eventually, and demand the truth. Although his answer may ruin your life. You may even have to kill him.

Late

HARRY GLOWER FIGURED he was seeing things again. In his rearview mirror a dark funnel dragged the prairie like a panther's tail, while ahead of him to the west was a bright blue sky. It didn't seem possible, what he was seeing. But he kept glancing behind, feeling that familiar cramp in his gut that he'd felt before when he'd seen other incredible things: a three-headed chimp, a bat with a ten-foot wing-span. And worse. He'd just spent a month in a Florida rehab drying out after a long, unemployed winter. But now he was in a rush to catch up with the show, and he felt better, almost pure. Dry and pure. So, things shouldn't be chasing him. Sure, he'd dipped in the hooch a little last night in Tulsa—dipped bad, actually—had another nightmare, and didn't know where he was when he woke. Big fucking bat flying around in his room again. He'd gone out wandering the streets in his underwear, got pinched and had a hell of a time talking his way out of it. Okay, so he still had some poison in his system. But he was better. Better. Too much better to be seeing this tornado.

Harry hit the sauce every winter. The circus laid him off every fall, and he'd drift back to Jacksonville. But this spring the show took off without him, didn't wait for him to get out of the tank. Left without Harry the Strong Man whose job was to enter the ring where Shreelah, the scantily-clad acrobat rode the lion's back; and he'd raise them both on his shoulders. Lion and woman. He liked to proposition Shreelah while she was in the air. "Hey, Shreel, baby," he'd say, "I'll put you down again if you promise to meet me behind the freak tent."

And she'd say something like, "You ever had a lion shit on your head?" All the while smiling at the crowd, arms in the air.

But right now he wished he could say anything to her. Anything.

A long gulp from his bottle of mineral water, another glance at that weird thing in his mirror. Take the blue highways to avoid the state patrols. No license, no insurance. Just don't get anxious and blow the speed limit, okay? Hardly a house out in these parts. Hardly another car. Unsure where the show was now. In Shawnee this week? He wouldn't touch a drop of booze all summer if he could just catch them, talk one-on-one with Boss Marceau: "Look, Marce, I'm here. Remember me? Strong Man? I'm flat broke. Don't send me away. Please!"

What if Marceau wiggled his mustache and said in his fractured English, "It has been told me zat you walk out of loony house, but no doctor release you. Hmmm?" Well, in that case he'd claim some bureaucratic snafu, show him his release-slip from last year on which he'd done some crafty alterations to make it read this year.

But now this funnel-cloud was growing larger behind him. He'd never seen one of those ugly things in person before. What power! If it was real, maybe that explained why he met no cars: folks out here knew it was coming and ran for the shelters. The sky in his mirror purpled like a great bruise, like the ones that covered his body when the mission workers had found him under a bridge in Jacksonville last winter.

He missed hanging with the circus folks, playing poker till dawn with Rubber Man, with Etienne the lion-tamer, and 700-pound Georgio, a black man, so bloated he had to wrap his legs and sides with three miles of Ace Bandages in order to fit through doors. Sometimes after devouring a ten-pound steak and a kettle of spuds for a bedtime snack, Georgio would say, "Come here, Strong Man," and grabbing Harry, would toss him in the air like a baby. Harry loved those folks, they were his family, they would be glad to see him.

Then a thought struck: If Georgio could toss him so easily, ten feet in the air, Marceau might have tapped him to step into his Strong Man act: Georgio hoisting Shreelah and her lion. Maybe propositioning her, too. But she wouldn't, would she? She couldn't, he's too big, right? Harry tromped on the gas.

Fuel needle settling low. He saw a gas station at a four corners, and screeched to the pumps. Closed. Precious seconds shaking a few drops out of the hoses. He almost got down and sucked on them. Now the purple sky was over him. If this station was closed, this tornado must be a real dragon. The real McCoy. Or was this Sunday? People out here closed their businesses on Sundays, didn't they? And went off to church, right?

In his mirror the tornado tore up a whole section of fence at once, coiling it around in the air until it resembled one of those DNA models like the doctor had in his office. Art, he'd called it. "This," he'd said, "is what made you a trouble maker from the beginning."

Harry had laughed. "The story of my life?"

Doc shook his head. "Just the first roll of the dice, that's all. You have to keep rolling."

Sort of like Marceau's screwy holograph roulette wheel, a spinning spectre for the suckers and the maladroit, a coiling figure of bad luck.

He wondered if he should stop and bang on a farmer's door. But, hell, a house would explode if a tornado whacked it. So, outrun it! Zig zag! Yes, zig- zaggie-zig, down a side road to another side-road, and another. Until he was out of gas.

Harry got out of the car, stood facing TORNADO. It approached slowly now, roaring, ripping up sod and trees and chewing them in its great black mouth. In its coils, he saw tractors, fences, cows, grange halls, bibles, pulpits, hay-wagons, crop-dusting airplanes— all the stuff a tornado could eat in a mid-western swath. But also he saw some of his Florida pals going around and around: Three-Headed Chimp, Big Bat, Cyclops, Great Bearded Hog, and Hydra. They loved him, even if the show didn't love him anymore.

Or maybe they weren't really there. But they were. If they loved him they must be there.

He threw his coat on the trunk, kicked off his shoes, pulled off his clothes and left them in a pile on the road. "I'm pure," he hollered, walking naked toward TORNA-DO, waving his arms. Finally breaking into a run.

Boss Hart

He should have talked to somebody before he went on TV. He should have told that woman who was after him that he wanted to fight it out in a regular court. A petty claims court, or something like that. Anybody could have told him his personality wasn't made for the tube, to say nothing of his looks. But Boss Hart wasn't close enough to anybody who would dare tell him. Definitely not close enough to us guys who worked construction for him. Even off hours, when he was Swinging Boss Hart, leader of a band called The Country Romancers, nobody knew him well enough to even bring up the subject.

I came home from work one day and my wife goes, "Don't your foreman have a belly dancer tattoo over his right eye, and a hawk feather or something braided into his hair on one side of his head?"

I go, "You mean Hart?"

She goes, "Yeah." She remembered meeting him at the Grasso Construction Company Christmas party and wasn't favorably impressed. "He's gonna be on TV tomorrow, on *Judge Rhonda*. I saw the previews today. She's gonna destroy him, Cary."

"You're pulling my leg, right?"

"No. This old girlfriend of his is suing him for back room and board. Guys like him don't last one round in her court."

Then I remembered Hart had taken a couple days off the week before. So, he must have driven down to the city for this *Judge Rhonda* thing. He'd probably never seen the show himself because he was always on the job weekdays, and didn't know he was driving toward the slaughter. I'd seen the show myself once when I was home with a twisted ankle, and Cindy was right: Rhonda was a man-eating shark, plain and simple, and she loved it when she got some idiot like Hart in front of her.

In fact we'd all noticed he'd come back from his days off a little more peevish than usual, making me work in hot blacktop up to my chest, making another guy scrub out the portable johns while he banged on the outside of them with a sledge hammer, putting other guys on all-day jackhammer duty unless they gave him half their lunches, sticking an air hose down a guy's pants. It got us talking union at the time. But we didn't understand the cause of his bad humor.

I phoned the rest of the guys and told them what was coming. We all called in sick the next day and took a quarter keg over to Lee's house to party and watch Boss Hart get creamed by a woman TV judge. With all of us out sick, Hart would be alone out on the work site. Maybe he'd stick an air hose down his own pants. But I figured he'd asked for it.

Well, the show was a nightmare for Hart. By my count, Judge Rhonda told him to shut up twenty-three times, to hush nineteen times. Asked him if he'd ever had brain surgery, and when he said no, told him he'd better hurry up and do so. Asked him where the rest of his feathers went. And was that a picture of his mother over his right eye, or his father? Boss Hart was reduced to a sobbing rubble. Plus she ordered him to pay $2,782.50 to his old squeeze who left the court with her nose in the air.

When it was over we kind of looked at our beers and didn't say anything for awhile. We found him an hour later out at the worksite, sitting on a big coil of cable, his hard hat in his lap, looking dumb and empty as an old shoe with the laces open. Staring at a pile of crushed stone. We drove right up to him in Lee's jeep.

I go, "Get in, Boss." He stood up without a word and climbed into the backseat like he was going to his execution.

We took him out and bought him one of those old fashioned watches you wear on a chain. We all chipped in for it. I don't know why the hell we did that. Nor do I know for sure why, on the following Saturday, we took our wives to see Swinging Boss Hart and the County Romancers. As mean as he'd been to us. The wives weren't excited about it, but we had a good time dancing and he was glad to see us and bought us about ten rounds. He did have a sweet side, we found out.

Things were better on the job for most of a month. Then they started downhill again. He made me trowel cement with my bare hands. He punished Lee by nailing the toes of his shoes to a board—and counter-sunk them—so he couldn't go to coffee break with the rest of us. Then he slammed Johnny Miller's lunch box shut on his tongue. Got us talking union again.

When I told my wife, she goes, "This must be the week he's gotta mail in the certified check."

And I go, "That explains it."

Then she goes, "But what do you put up with it for?"

She always asks the hard questions.

The Fish Burglars

BUSTING INTO HOUSES at night was getting harder all the time. Used to be you could pick a lock, any lock, they were easy, and you were in. If no one stirred, you grabbed the TV, took whatever else looked interesting, and you were out. But things were changing—people were getting more crime conscious, crime wise, and crime weary. Bobo and Latch both noticed it. Locks were getting more complicated. People slept lighter—the slightest sound and a whole family was awake and out of bed, trying to beat your head in with a ball bat, if not using something more lethal. Bobo knew they had to change their modus or they were out of business.

He came up with the idea of tying fish to the soles of their shoes so they could slip more quietly in and out of houses at night. It worked for awhile. But then the cops caught on that two guys were busting into apartments with fish tied to their shoes, leaving trails of scales. Detectives staked out city fish markets, watching for two men buying four catfish at a time, or four trout, or haddock, whatever was fresh. They had to be fresh or the stink would wake people up. People were stink conscious. A lot of innocent guys got picked up just for walking into places like Jimmy's Fresh Seafood on 18th St., and buying four fish.

Probably Bobo and Latch got away with it as long as they did because they each bought two fish, and paid for them separately, an hour apart. Or, once in awhile Latch would buy one fish and Bobo would buy three. Or they'd buy eight fish and put four in the fridge for another night. Their strongest suit was always their unpredictability. Anyway, they knew the heat was on, and they finally quit doing it. But while it lasted it was one of the best ideas Bobo ever had.

One night they went into a second floor apartment walking on fish, and never made a sound except the pin in the lock and the creak of the door hinges, most of which they silenced with fish oil. A big round moon shined through the windows and made a perfectly illuminated path down the hallway through the apartment to the living room where they could see the TV, a 17-inch Quasar. They knew this tube well, they'd swiped and sold it a dozen times at least. And the stubborn owner kept buying it back from some fence.

Bobo's hands were almost on the tube when they heard a voice, and they froze in place, and turned to make their exit. But the voice was coming from the open door of a room that was between them and the outside door.

"I told you, baby," came a man's voice, "I smell fish."

A woman's voice answered, "Then you got a smeller like a hound dog, 'cause there ain't no fish in this house.

You must be smellin' something clear down the street."

Then the two voices commenced arguing, which in this situation was almost as good as them being asleep since no one hears well while arguing. Bobo unplugged the set and Latch hoisted the TV into his arms. They tiptoed back down the silver moon path, past the room where the couple was arguing, and walked smack into a small kid who tumbled backward onto the floor, then leapt back onto his feet like a cat.

The thud got the attention of the two arguers.

"Desmond, is that you?" called the woman.

"Mamma," the kid screamed. "It's them men with fish on their shoes."

The apartment exploded in battle. When Bobo tried to remember it all later, he recalled picking up a kitchen chair and beaning the man with it, then using it to fend off the woman who had a kitchen knife in her hand, or what looked like a knife, since it was too dark to tell. He held the chair with one hand and threw a toaster at her with the other, then a Mr. Coffee. But this woman was coming at him all the same.

That was also the night Bobo found out how well you can run on fish—not well. They're so slippery you seem to be running in place, like a Michael Jackson dance on fast-forward. When the police finally showed up they shined their lights on the getaway path, which illuminated a trail of scales, but they found only four badly squeezed monkfish on the sidewalk where Bobo and Latch had cut them free with a pocketknife.

After they'd jumped a few fences, Bobo and Latch slowed to a saunter. "We gotta come up with a new tune,"

Bobo said, catching his breath.

"Maybe we go barefoot next time," Latch suggested.

"Nah, we need our shoes," Bobo said. "How about strip steaks?"

"Ain't hungry," Latch said.

"No, nitwit. I mean we tie strip steaks to the bottom of our shoes."

Latch thought for a moment. "Then we better cook 'em first, or we'll leave a trail of blood."

"That's okay, man," Bobo said. "That's what we do. Yessir, that's what we do."

The Brave Dog

After Ernest Hemingway's story, "The Faithful Bull"

THERE WAS A dog, and he was a brave dog, and his name was not King or Caesar or Ben Hur, or any of the bad names that people, usually men, give to dogs. He was a brave dog and he fought other dogs, and he fought well. He was solitary, and did not socialize with other dogs. He never looked for a fight, but he was always ready to battle, and he never ran away, and he never lost a fight. For this reason his owner, who owned many dogs, took him to dogfights in backyards, in dark lots behind old warehouses, and even out in the woods. Other dogs were afraid of him, but they were brave dogs too, and they did not run away from him in fights. His owner bet money on him, and all the men who bet money on him went away with their pockets bulging because he was a great dog and a great fighter.

But soon he was running out of dogs to fight. The dogs that men sent to fight him were beaten badly. Sometimes a dog that was worth five hundred dollars before a fight was worth only two hundred dollars after the fight. And sometimes dogs were worth only fifty dollars after he fought them, and some were worth nothing at all. So, the owner could not make any more money on him because the dog had fought too well. He was brave. But he had fought too well.

So the owner decided to board the dog with a woman he knew. He asked the woman to take the dog in and she agreed. It was a good home, and the woman had many dogs of her own and was kind to them. The owner hoped that if he kept the dog out of fights for awhile he might calm down, breed with the female dogs that the woman owned, and become less introverted and less vicious instead of ruining the owner's business.

But this did not work. The dog was not interested in socializing with the woman's dogs because they were docile and bored him, and because he fell in love with the woman. The woman did not understand this at first, and kept trying to socialize him, encouraging him to breed with the other dogs. Sometimes she even held up the tails of some of the female dogs and pointed, but he was not interested because he loved only the woman. He loved the woman with all the focus and strength with which he had once fought dogs. This unnerved the woman when she finally realized it, and she made many frantic phone calls to the owner. She had to shake him off her leg, and he constantly jumped on her bed at night. But what truly unnerved her was his look of unmitigated ardor, following her from room to room.

So the owner took the dog back. He did not know what to do with the dog now, so he put the dog in fights again. But now the dog did not fight well because he was in love, fully and completely, and now he would fight only for love. He would not fight for any other reason. Only for love, and certainly not for money or glory. The owner did not understand this, and the dog's refusal to fight baffled and frustrated him. When he sent the dog into the first fight he was worth a thousand dollars, but after the fight he was worth only two hundred and fifty dollars, and after the next fight he was worth only ten or twelve dollars and change.

Early in the morning after the last fight the owner tied the dog to a lamppost outside the Humane Society, knowing that the people at the Humane Society would take him in when they came to work and found him tied up. He knew that they would put him in a cage and feed him and try to find a new owner, but that they would not find a new owner, and the dog would have to be killed.

The woman who killed the dog was a brave woman. She killed many dogs, sometimes several in a single day because she was a good woman and knew that the dogs no longer had a place in the world and therefore would only suffer. She injected a syringe with potassium chloride into the meat of the dog's shoulder which stopped his heart. The dog died swiftly, and without great pain.

But the owner, meanwhile, could not stop thinking about the dog, and finally he called the pound. He did not realize that the woman he spoke to on the phone was the very one who had killed the dog, and she did not tell him that fact. But she told him that he had called too late. Your dog is dead, she told him.

He was a good dog, the owner sobbed. Kind and faithful.

No doubt, she said. Most dogs are.

Faithful, he repeated.

Perhaps, she said, we should all be like dogs.

Cows' Eyes

DURING THE SPRING that his marriage broke up, Jerry cobbled together a temporary living that would see him through the summer. He began teaching a class in Eastern religion at the state college in the afternoons, and mornings he worked for Dr. Edna Carnahan in the Biology Department, dissecting cows' eyes. He didn't know anything about biology, or the purpose of her project, and he didn't need to; all that the job entailed was using a microscope and a fine blade to cut, carefully, a tiny gem of lens from each orb while it stared back at him gloomily. And dropping the lens into alcohol. Then going on to the next eye, and the next. Also, once each week, he drove to a slaughterhouse for a new supply of cows' eyes, which came in cardboard buckets like Col. Sanders' chicken. That was the best part of his week, the trip to the slaughterhouse out in the country, fifty miles south. He drove with his windows down, even on some unseasonably chilly June mornings.

He wasn't sure why the eyes' gazes bothered him when he dissected them. They weren't connected to a cow anymore and, in fact, cows meant nothing special to him. A city-raised man, he'd never actually touched a cow. He was pretty sure they were female (since they gave milk), but they seemed like androgynous blobs to him.

By the second week of class he was having a problem with one of his students, named Paula, a few years older than the others, who laughed at everything. She sparred with him about the meaning of Buddhist rituals and chants, such as The Four Vows, as if she expected him to defend them. "How can one person save all beings?" she groaned, in reference to the First Vow. "Why would anyone vow to do something impossible? Aren't we already expected to do enough impossible things?" Another day she butted heads with him on the Buddhist principle of dependent co-arising. Her voice carried the hint of a taunt. She had tied back her usually tangled hair, as if in preparation for some kind of sword-crossing, and she rubbed her bare feet together under her chair the way people rub their hands when they're having wicked fun. "Would you mind explaining it again?" she asked.

Jerry cleared his throat, conscious of a barely audible but exasperated exhalation from some of the other students. "Well," he said, trying to remember how he had explained it the day before, and rubbing his own hands in thought, "it's the idea that we're responsible for whatever happens. Good or ill. By participating in life we assume co-responsibility."

She shook her head and demanded an illustration. It was finally coming to him that she got a charge out of flustering him.

He said, "I guess, if you went into the cafeteria here and ate a hot dog, and got sick from it, the food service company would be responsible, but you would also be responsible for eating it."

"Doesn't sound fair," she said.

"Well," he shrugged, "you do know what goes into hot dogs." He immediately thought of cows' eyes; didn't eyes go into hot dogs? "And anyway, it's not about fairness."

By eight o'clock that night Jerry was in Hennigan's, drinking drafts and reading the text, trying to stay at least two concepts ahead of the class, trying to get enough read in case Paula came in again and sat across from him at his table, and took the book out of his hands.

* * *

He dreamed vividly that summer, and one night he dreamed that he was walking after dark in the village park with his wife Diana; there was a crowded Ferris wheel, smoke, and a medley of savory aromas. In his dream they were still together, and she had drawn his hand into the front pouch of her parka, where she held it warmly. The most intelligent person he'd ever known. In his dream she wasn't suing him for the house and the car. Nor was he infatuated with Paula. And in the dark sky, high above the wheel, the melancholy moon was a great cow's eye, rolling through the clouds, sadly watching the carnival. Lovers looked at the moon and laughed and mooed.

But mostly his dreams were more upsetting. They woke him in his dark room and he lay awake watching the dream-images fade in the blackness as if neon was ebbing out of them.

One Friday morning he came down to his car to realize that he'd left it unlocked and someone had been in it during the night. The window was down. Pages had been torn from his spiral notebook, and wadded into dozens of balls and tossed onto the seat and floor. He unwadded one of them expecting to see his own notes, but found someone's anonymous scribbles, attempts to write something and repeatedly messing it up. Then he found one sheet that was folded and sticking out of his ashtray. It read, almost illegibly, *Damn can't say the right damn thng—too late too drunk can't think. Breakfast w/ me?*

* * *

Jerry sat at the microscope, staring into a cow's eye, lifting the lens with the tip of the blade. I will stay away from Paula, he promised himself. He said it to the eye. Goddamn it. He left the lab early that day to study the text, so that after lunch he came to class better prepared than he had been since the beginning of the course. He walked hurriedly down the hallway to the classroom, the squeak of his shoes echoing.

This was the day he was to talk about koans. To his dismay, he found that three women from the class had formed an evening discussion group; they had been meeting while he'd been sitting in Hennigan's with Paula. One of them stopped him on his way into class and told him about the group, pushing her glasses up on her nose as she spoke. In the first half hour of the class he realized the three women were far ahead of the others, even ahead of him. When he tried to explain a koan to Paula, who as usual pressed him for meaning, one of the students said, "A Zen monk asks his master if a dog has Buddha nature, and the master answers, *Mu!*"

"Moo!" Paula laughed at her. "You mean, moo like a cow?"

"No," the student answered, clearly irked, "it's spelled m-u, the word means 'nothing'."

"And that's the answer to the koan?" Paula scoffed. "Nothing?"

"No, that's just the meaning of the word," she replied. "The answer to the koan is beyond verbal explanation. It only comes with concentration."

"Oh...hell," Paula answered, and looked out the window.

Yes, hell, Jerry thought. Hell in the morning and afternoon, a little ecstasy in the evening—because he couldn't stay away from Paula. Then more hell for dreams.

* * *

The next morning Jerry went to pick up another bucket of cows' eyes. He left home before dawn, so that he'd be back in time to dissect a few more eyes before he had to go to class. He felt an urgency now to finish the project, although Dr. Carnahan wasn't telling him how many more eyes she wanted him to dissect. A few hundred, a few thousand, a hundred thousand? "Getting tired?" she'd asked. He'd said he wasn't. Nope. In fact it wasn't tiredness he felt, not in the usual sense of the word. It was just that whenever he pierced an eye with the blade its pupil would suddenly contract—the way his own pupils narrowed in his bathroom mirror when he turned on the light. Or, it seemed to. He wasn't sure if it was really happening or if it was an illusion, but it made him feel that he was inflicting pain, as if the eye itself was a sentient being. And that was making him edgy.

He shut off his engine in the parking lot of the slaughterhouse, and listened to the radio for a few minutes, watching the sun burn the dew from cars that looked like they had been sitting in the lot all night. He listened to the news, and to a couple songs, and smoked a cigarette. Although he was sitting outside a death house for cows, the morning was beautiful. He could see a double track-head that connected the railroad to the slaughterhouse, and a couple of rail cars with their doors open so he could see through them to the woods beyond.

It occurred to him that in all his trips down here, he had never seen an actual cow at the slaughterhouse, being led in. Maybe they were brought in at night in those rail cars, mooing their heads off.

"What do you do with all them eyes, fella?" a bloody-aproned clerk at the slaughterhouse asked him while pressing the lid down tight on the bucket.

"Ping-pong," Jerry answered, tiredly.

The clerk laughed. And it suddenly came to Jerry, as he carried the bucket out to his car and placed it on the seat, that he envied the clerk. The clerk's life must be uncomplicated, even if awash in blood, or he wouldn't laugh this early in the morning, especially at something that was only mildly funny. The thing that he admired most was that the clerk was just a slaughterhouse employee. Or, so he appeared. Not two or three non-integratable things. Like an eye-dissector and a religion teacher, as well as a philanderer, and a defendant (he'd been served papers a few days before; Diana wasn't fooling around, she was really suing).

On the road Jerry listened to the radio again. He played the oldies station, and tried not to think. Then a silly old song came on: *Paula, I can't wait no more for you, my love.* "Mawkish crap," he snorted and switched the station, but landed on a religious station with a barking preacher, and it startled him as if he'd opened a wrong door somewhere and met a mean dog. He shut the radio off.

As he drove through an area of woods and cornfields he saw a flash of movement to his right, and a buck deer and a doe bounded across the road. Jerry jammed the brakes, skidding sideways. The bucket launched from the seat and exploded against the dashboard, eyes bouncing everywhere inside the car, eyes hitting him in the face, slapping against the windshield, rolling along the dashboard, dropping in his lap, and into his crotch. Jerry pulled to the roadside, and gasped for breath. And when he opened his left hand he was clutching an eye. Slowly he got out of the car, opening all the doors, finding eyes under the seat, everywhere. An eye rolled under the car when he opened the passenger-side door. He spat on a handkerchief and wiped the grit off of some of them, dropping them back in the cardboard bucket with little plunking sounds until they covered the cardboard bottom; after that the sounds were so utterly soft—pith, pith—that he heard them only because he knew he was dropping them.

When he got back into the car his knees still felt like jelly from fright, and he could barely operate the pedals. He sat for a few minutes, then he reached his cell phone from his pocket and dialed Paula. Her number was ringing before he remembered how early it was, and that she wasn't an early riser.

"Yeah?" came her thick voice. When he spoke to her, she said, "Baby, that's you? You sound crazy."

He took a deep breath and told her about hitting the breaks and cow's eyes flying all over.

She said, "Baby, you had a bad dream?"

The question stumped him for a moment. Then he remembered that he'd told her very little about what he did for Dr. Carnahan, and probably never told her that he went on weekly runs for buckets of cows' eyes. "No," he said, "it isn't a dream."

She was silent for a moment, then she said, "It's not, huh? Then is this like, what's it called, co-dependence rising?"

"Something like that," he told her. Then he added, "No, no. Not at all. I'm responsible, no one else. Forget all that goddamn Buddhist stuff right now." He realized he was still breathing hard.

"So, like...what do you want me to do about it?"

He didn't answer. He put the phone back in his pocket, and started his car. The eyes were back in their bucket, and his heart took a breath. Ten or twelve miles up the road the woods and cornfields disappeared, and he found himself in wide grazing land, barbed wire fences. Hundreds of placid bovines, chewing. Cows are only cows, probably unknowable beasts. Jerry wondered if anyone had ever tried to ride a cow like a horse, or even like a rodeo steer. He was sure it couldn't be done successfully, or he would have seen someone doing it in a movie. But some fools must try from time to time. Fools are with us always.

The Block

THE BENCHES WERE hard, and the floor was filthy. Martin found himself sitting next to a woman a few years younger than himself, someone he might have wanted to get to know under different circumstances. Her name was Kay, her fingers were ringless like his own, and she was dressed in a pair of worn-out Dockers, a sweat shirt, and grass-stained sneakers. But, if her red hair weren't so tangled, he thought she would be attractive. He knew he looked at least as disheveled as she. On the other side of the door, the crowd was roaring in excitement, and even laughing.

"How'd you get here?" he asked her.

"You gotta ask?" Kay replied.

He held out his cigarette pack, but she refused. Signs said they weren't supposed to smoke in this room, though several people were, and the guard who was dressed like a movie usher was ignoring the infractions.

"Yes, I've got to ask," he said. "What else is there to talk about?"

Kay shrugged. "My daughter got sick—that's her

sitting over there. She's okay now, though she don't talk to me no more."

"Sick with what?"

"What didn't she have! Started with a rheumatic heart, and it went downhill from there. Been in the hospital more times than I can count. They fixed her up. But, you know. What about you?"

"Lost my business," he said.

"That all?" she asked.

"No," he said, "there were similar medical expenses. But it was me—I was the sick one."

She shook her head. "Mind me asking how much debt?"

"Couple hundred grand," he said, "after they took my house. What about you?"

"Forty grand and change."

"That's all?"

"Sure," she said, "but it was all on credit cards. Insurance didn't cover nothing after I got laid off. So I sold the house and the car to pay off the hospital. Then we couldn't do nothing but live on the cards. But they raised those to 19.99%"

The guard opened the door and called a man named Lang, who got up and crushed his cigarette under his shoe and then shuffled through the door. The guard shut the door behind him.

"It's hot in here," she said.

"It sure as hell is," Martin said. "When did they come after you?"

"Oh god," she said. "Which ones? State Central Bank made the first claim and sent me up to Fargo, North

Dakota. I sat there for two weeks before they decided to move us all down to Chicago. But I guess they wanted way too much. Trying to get their money back. More'n I was worth, I guess. So then NewBank got hold of me and sent me down here to Wilmington. You?"

"NewBank sent me here, too. In fact I had three NewBank cards." He chuckled. But it didn't feel good to chuckle—it made his belly jiggle and he didn't want her to notice how paunchy he was. Though he didn't really know why he cared. What difference could it make now?

"I guess we're pretty near the ocean," Kay said, looking around the room as if she ought to be able to see the Atlantic through the walls. "Tell you the truth, this is close as I ever got to the ocean. I ain't had many vacations."

There was a roar from the crowd beyond the door.

Martin said, "What's your last name?"

She smirked. "Pierson. What's yours?"

"Martin."

"Guess you come before me, then. Fact, you might even be next."

He supposed she was right. Lang had just gone. He'd gotten to know Lang on the bus to Wilmington. Lang had never smoked before the trip, but now he smoked incessantly, bumming cigarettes from everyone as if he had a death wish. Now Martin wondered how Lang was making out. Poor debt-ridden bastard. This seemed harder on him than anyone else. But Martin wouldn't get the opportunity to ask about Lang. Probably he'd never see Lang again, nor anyone else he'd traveled with.

After a few minutes the door opened and the guard said, "Martin."

Martin said goodbye to Kay, and walked slowly through the door and onto the block, or what they called "the block," although it was really just a stage in a small movie house.

"Stand out in the light," a voice hollered to him in a nasal southern twang. Looking to his left, Martin saw the auctioneer approaching him with a print-out on a clipboard.

Martin's eyes slowly adjusted so that he could see. The theater was about a third filled with bidders. Some looked bored. On the left rear of the theater near the door, two men sat at a table with a laptop, and Martin knew they must be the NewBank reps.

"Name is Carl W. Martin," said the auctioneer. "Fifty-one years old. Now, he's a little overweight, as you can plainly see. And these new lemon laws that come down from Washington say I gotta give you an honest and fair assessment. Moderately high blood pressure, near-sighted, prostate the size of a sweet potato. But now, listen folks: His I.Q. is 131 and three quarters. He can fix your computer, cook a mean hollandaisy sauce. Speaks French. And he can recite 'The Charge of the Light Brigade' for your dinner guests."

A few titters went through the audience. Martin let his shoulders slump until the auctioneer delivered a sharp slap across his back.

"NewBank sets the minimum bid at fifteen thousand. Do I hear twenty?"

Martin wondered how Kay was going to make out. What her minimum bid would be. And her daughter's. He wondered where he was going now. And he wondered why he wondered.

Clone

LIKE A LOT of people, Nancy was intrigued by a news
story about a woman who had cloned her dead cat. And
how the cat-clone was, in every respect, just like the
one she'd lost a year before, except new, youthful, with
a new lease. Nancy read the story several times, carried
the newspaper to the coffee shop and read it again over
a hazelnut au lait, trying to decide what to do about this
new twist of science. The woman in the news story was a
lonely widow. And Nancy was a lonely widow. So, for her,
the story had grit.

Nancy's last marriage had been her third and most
unhappy marriage, all three of which were to Max Coover.
Not that any of her marriages to him were fun. But the
third was the worst. Her shrink had explained to her late-
ly that she'd unwittingly had her antenna up all her life
for a loud, authoritative, unfeeling man—which satisfied
some odd emptiness in Nancy that she could never fill on
her own, nor with the few milquetoast men she'd been
with in between marriages to Coover. But Coover was the
model of domestic belligerence. Her shrink had been try-

ing to convince Nancy to divorce him, once again and for all.

Nancy had been going for long walks around the park, praying and thinking about it. She'd been right on the verge of a decision when his boss called and told her that Coover had been taken to the hospital with a heart attack. He was dead before she got there. Well, actually, she'd taken a few detours. She'd even stopped at Pet Smart and looked at cats. Stuck her finger in some of the cages. "Kiss-kiss," she'd said, and let them rub their faces against her knuckles. She'd looked at a dozen more cats in the glass front window that reflected back her lean, bespectacled face; and she'd pulled herself away when she realized that she'd stopped looking at the cats, and only at her reflection, at the cold parking lot reflected in it.

The first thing she did, even before the funeral, was to put Moby down—Max's idiotic, mean, and even dangerous pit bull terrier. It had had one red, runny eye. The stupid mutt had even killed Killian, her old cat, the one she was now thinking of cloning. Well, he hadn't actually killed Killian. But he had certainly shortened her life by slobbering all over her, rolling her over like a ball with his nose, picking her up by the nape of her neck and dropping her into the toilet.

The cloning was going to take time, a woman scientist at the InStar Clinic told her. And big bucks, too, every dime of the thirty thousand she'd gotten from Coover's triple indemnity life insurance.

How long had her cat been dead? asked the woman. The stains on her lab coat intrigued Nancy. Were these stains from other cats in the making?

"Only a year," Nancy told her, holding her breath for fear the scientist would say, Sorry, it has been too long. But she only said that it was going to be harder, that Nancy would have to search her house for some remaining cells of her old cat: hair, nail clippings, anything. But those things were already dust that she knew she'd vacuumed long ago.

It was hopeless, and she gave up on the idea until one morning, while searching her closet for her winter shoes, she found an old pillow that had formerly served as Killian's bed. There must be cells in that old thing, she thought. An hour later she was in the lab again, and the same scientist was handling the pillow with rubber gloves.

"We'll need a check in advance," the scientist warned. "You'll get a call from us when the animal is ready to go home with you."

Contracts were signed in triplicate, and Nancy wrote the big check. But so much time passed that she often forgot about it. Christmas came and went, and just before Easter she got a call from InStar. Her pet was six weeks old, they told her, and ready to go home. Nancy raced to the clinic with her cat carrier on the seat of the car, even passing Pet Smart again, thinking of those other cats that wouldn't do. She'd call this one Killian, again. It was expensive getting one's quality of life back. But it could be done.

The scientist met her in the waiting room, and led her back to a little zoo-smelling holding area, and disappeared through flapping double doors while Nancy waited. Finally the woman returned with a puppy in her arms.

"What?" Nancy stammered in alarm. "What is that?"

"Cute, isn't it?" said the scientist. "But it already has the unmistakable pit bull characteristics."

In the shouting match that followed, Nancy demanded her money back. Her contract was brought out and it was shown to her that the clinic had promised no specific result. And it was explained that this dog was cloned from cells isolated from the pillow she'd provided. Now, in Nancy's mind's eye, she saw the pillow as it had been carried through her house in the drooling jaws of that awful dog she'd put down.

"Your name will be Coover, by the way," she told the dog riding home in the car seat beside her, noticing for the first time its red, runny eye. "We're going to make the best of this, damn it. I paid thirty thousand for you, and you are going to be called Coover. And let's get this straight right now: You are going to do whatever I say."

Increase

The first significant crime in more than sixty years in the village of Increase, New York occurred some few weeks before Y2K when a young man named Stanley Stankly robbed the public library. Stanley lived in a single-storey rental house on the edge of Increase, and had a pro-bono lawyer fighting his eviction on the grounds that he had nowhere else to go—no one would take Stanley in. For the record, he was paying his rent, more or less. But the village code enforcer had determined that Stanley's house was so termite-infested that it was in danger of collapsing. Also, for the record, the library was in another termite-infested house, fighting eviction on the same grounds. No one would provide a new home for the library. Stanley and the library had the same lawyer, by the way.

    The robbery was meant to be a big joke. A girl that Stanley had gone to high school with, Marcie Monmouth (whose great, great, great grandfather, Increase Monmouth, was the village's namesake, although no one now recalls why it was called Increase instead of Monmouth), worked alone in the library on Wednesday evenings—the only evening that the library was open. Stanley had a life-long crush on Marcie Monmouth.

She was always sucking on sugar-free candy be-cause she had type-one diabetes; nevertheless, as often happens with severe diabetics, her teeth became so de-cayed that, the week after her eighteenth birthday, her fa-ther drove her over the border to a Canadian dentist who pulled all her teeth in one appointment and gave her a complete set of false teeth. They went to Canada because no dentist in New York would perform such a procedure, at least not all her teeth at once.

Marcie wasn't fat like most diabetics; in fact she was quite tall and wiry. She was simply born with a bad pancreas. Stanley was fat, but he was healthy. When Mar-cie—still groggy from the sleeping gas— and her father came out of the dentist's office with her new ill-fitting teeth protruding in an absurd overbite, there was Stan-ley standing on the sidewalk, raising his hand and say-ing, "Hey, Marce!" She and her father were stunned that this village ne'er-do-well had followed them all the way to Canada. Without a word Mr. Mounmouth hustled his daughter into the car and drove away, as Stanley hollered after them, "I wanted to be first to tell you...." But his voice trailed off. He'd wanted to say she was stunning with her new teeth.

In fact, she looked terrible, and knew it, and she cried all the way home, and her father had to bring her back to Canada two days later for emergency adjustments to prevent her from killing herself.

On the night of the robbery, Stanley walked into the library at 8:21 PM—according to police reports—and said, "Hey, Marce!" to Marcie, who was behind the circulation desk. She gave him her usual barely-discernable nod. Marcie had a small face and a cascade of red hair that made her look like she was peeking through a wall of flames. Stanley pulled out a toy German Lugar and said, "Hand over your cash."

Stanley had been locally famous once before. One morning, when he was in the third grade at Increase Elementary, he'd simply disappeared from the school, inspiring a county-wide dragnet. But he turned up in the truant officer's own car where he'd gone, bashfully, and waited to be discovered. He had also pissed his pants by then, which was what most traumatized him about the incident. He might have become locally famous for his trip to Canada, but the Monmouths chose not to talk about that incident.

Yet now, for the second time in less than a year, Marcie was slack-jawed by something Stanley Stankly was doing, and she gaped at him. He wanted to say, "Nice teeth, Marce." But he didn't. She had gotten them adjusted by that time, so she didn't look so much like a redheaded barracuda.

Shocked and trembling, she handed over the overdue fines from the cash drawer, which that day had accumulated $9.40 in cash, and a few checks. Her sugar free candies fell out of her pocket in the process and scattered on the floor. Stanley refused the checks. Then with the cash in one hand, and the toy Lugar in the other, he asked her for a date. When she continued to stare at him, he said, "Just kidding, Marce. Sort of." And out he went, laughing to himself. He walked the two blocks home, shoved a tape into his VCR, and sat down to a *Lord of the Rings* episode (which, by the way, he'd borrowed from the library the day before), figuring he'd give the money back in the morning, and he'd laugh the whole thing off.

The movie credits had barely rolled when his front door was kicked in and two village cops entered with their weapons drawn. That was at 8:42 PM. Later, their reports claimed that Stanley had reached for a weapon, though no weapon of any description was ever found. Not even the toy. Anyway, they both opened fire. The bullets passed through the wall on either side of Stanley's head, and exploded the fuse box next to the refrigerator in the adjacent kitchen, pitching the house into darkness. More shots were fired. The house shook, and creaked like an old boat. One cop tumbled out the door, and ran to his car to call for reinforcements, while Stanley crawled through the dark looking for a way out.

Stanley had one other ally in the preservation of his house: the village historian, named Grace Reed Land. Although her interest had nothing to do with Stanley's wellbeing, but only that the house had been, briefly, the residence of Brigham Young, prior to his meeting Joseph Smith, prior his bevy of wives and his messianic mission to the west. Ms. Land simply wanted the house preserved, if possible on the National Landmark register.

At precisely 8:55 PM, by the library's clock, Stanley reentered the library, and found Marcie still at the counter with the register open, and the library's director, Ms. Colleen FitzPatrick, standing there with her coat on.

"Marce," Stanley said. "I was only kiddin' ya. Here's your money. And he slapped $9.20 on the counter.

He was profoundly shaken by the guns that had just been fired at his head, and his heart was pounding in his beefy chest like a washing machine out of balance, but he was holding himself together.

Stiffly, Ms. FitzPatrick counted the cash and said, "It's supposed to be $9.40."

Stanley fished in his jeans and came up with another quarter, and told Ms. FitzPatrick to keep the change.

At that moment, Marcie, who had been shaking like a windsock, broke into tears, at which Stanley picked up one of her sugar-free candies from the counter and handed it to her. But she swatted it away and it skidded over the floor. Stanley was still in the company of the two women at 9:07 when they locked the front door. He was still trying to pass it all off as a joke, apologizing in gushes, offering Marcie a Kleenex from the pocket of his jeans.

The police blockade was blazingly visible from the library's front porch, and the two women stopped and gasped at the sight. Neither woman was aware of what they had caused by having called the cops, or how it connected to Stanley. In fact, Ms. Fitzpatrick said, "What do you suppose is going on over there?" Later she would tell police that when Stanley returned to the library with the cash in hand, she'd assumed he was doing so on the advice of the police, and that that would be the end of the whole incident. She was stunned later when she learned of the shoot-out. Ms. FitzPatrick said a polite goodnight to Stanley and then drove Marcie home.

As he approached the blockade on foot, Stanley could see village, deputy, and state police cars parked in his front yard. Other towners were there, and the cops were trying to herd them back. Grace Reed Land was among them, as was Stanley's lawyer. His house seemed to be sinking into the basement like a houseboat succumbing to leaks. He had a Plexiglas ant farm in the basement, he had sensimilla plants under a sun lamp in his basement, and now it looked like he was going to lose everything. One cop had a bullhorn and was telling him to come out with his hands on top of his head. Ha! They thought he was still in there! In fact, he'd barely gotten out a kitchen window with bullets flying all over the place, wondering how a joke could have carried so many so far. This was what happened when you fucked with a Monmouth in Increase.

Stanley circled the edge of the crowd and the blockade, finally coming to a police car sitting in the shadow of Increase's last great elm. The elm probably could remember when Brigham Young lived in his house. He opened the door to the back seat, got in, and shut it. And waited.

"This is your final warning," the bull-horning cop was shouting at Stanley's sinking house. "Come out with your hands on your head, or we're coming in."

He heard glass breaking. They must be throwing tear gas into his house. Maybe that would get rid of those damned termites.

The Death of Johnny Red Heart

IN THE SUMMER of 1967, when I was between high school and college, I worked as a cook in a restaurant on the New York State Thruway, and one night there I watched a customer die. His name, and you may remember him, was Johnny Red Heart, or at least that was the name the world knew him by. If he hadn't been famous, it would still have made an enormous impression on me since I was a teenager and I'd never witnessed a death.

He'd arrived at The Holiday House—as those Thruway restaurants were called then—in a bus with his name painted in rope letters on the sides. He strode in dressed in black, his yellow hair slicked back, with an entourage of musicians and roadies in cowboy hats. Stopped and kissed a couple babies. Hollered, "Howdy-doo folks," and other such absurdities. Even as a northerner I could tell his Texas twang was embellished.

It was around 8:30 in the evening, which seemed significant because his new song, "Twilight," had hit the charts—what we would now call a crossover hit, meaning that both rock and country stations were playing it every few minutes. The song went: "I'm gonna change for you baby, just you wait if you don't believe. Watch me in the twilight. Bad boy's gonna change." A mawkish song of idiotic promises, but people loved it, cried over it. He wasn't liked by the critics who called him the most derivative country star that ever took the stage at the Rineman Theatre. They said he just stole a bit of every country star and added a big dose of sex.

In fact, that summer he had a much-ballyhooed paternity suit on his back. Southern lawyers in string ties were chasing him. Sometimes even police were after him. Yet he sang on, smearing the tabloids with his trademark grin, a little like one you would see on a tourist-trap totem pole: at once striking, unsettling, and comic. Today you remember his rakish grin as much as any of his songs.

Waitresses rushed him. Men scowled. But I should point out that such a visit wasn't really unusual in that restaurant. After all, celebrities use the Thruway too. They have to eat and pee like anyone else. Just a week before, I'd made cinnamon toast for Mitch Miller and I'd seen The Lovin' Spoonful slouching out of the men's room.

You probably think that I killed Johnny Red Heart with my cooking, that a famous all-night party animal and heartland libertine succumbed to some rancid secret burger sauce. But in fact he hadn't taken a bite yet. His order of six poached eggs and catsup on a quadruple serving of mashed potatoes and a side of strawberry shortcake—you remember an order like that even if the customer isn't famous—was still in the service window when I happened to see him slump over his table, burying his face in his Thruway place mat. I thought he was laughing, but he didn't straighten up. Then a commotion erupted around him, and his retinue dragged him, spurs jingling, into the kitchen hollering for smelling salts. We didn't have any such thing. They hollered for ammonia and someone went looking for a porter to find some. Somebody hollered for brandy. And someone had the sense to call an ambulance.

I left burgers burning on the grill to go and stand near where Johnny lay, while his friends stood around helplessly. And then I witnessed the most amazing thing. I watched his face relax. I mean, relax so much in dying that it was like he became a different man. Or several different men. The rake smile vanished, of course. But the rest of his public puss went with it, and he became Johnny Cash, then Ferlin Husky, Porter Wagoner, Bill Monroe, changing into one after another, and a whole bunch more Nashville golden throats, men who had big red American hearts, who could say hello with all the down-dirty of a moo cow.

I was dumb-struck. I said, "Hey, what's going on here?"

One musician looked at me like I was daft. "What's it look like?" he snapped. "You never seen a heart attack before?" Wasn't he seeing what I saw?

Johnny's face continued changing, reminding me of an old episode of the *Twilight Zone* (There goes that "twilight" thing again), where a man magically took other people's faces in order to commit crimes, but when he died his face morphed through the whole gallery of faces that he'd assumed.

Now Johnny Red Heart became Johnny Paycheck, Hank Garland, Ernie Tubb, Tex Ritter, Red Foley, Roy Acuff, Hank Williams, and Johnny Horton in one big finale, as he fought for breath. And then he lay still.

His band and roadies walked slowly out to the bus, where they were still standing around smoking when the manager sent me out with complimentary coffee, their faces hard and drawn. Their big hearts broken.

The Ninth Step

THE NINTH STEP was to make amends. The theory being that, if he didn't patch things up with people he had wronged, guilt would poison the eleven other steps. Everything would go to hell. Or at least that is what the Twelve Step people told him. He might even start drinking again, and Jay couldn't risk that. So, he went and apologized to his ex-wife, then he drove to his daughter's apartment, then over to his sisters' houses. No one took it very well. None wanted to talk about it or be apologized to. By late morning, when he was finally driving up Graham Road, he'd left a wake of people, stunned and crying. They didn't get it.

It was early spring, Graham was a muddy dirt road, and Jay had to creep carefully around the wash-outs. He could barely remember this road from five years before; he hadn't been up here again in all that time. Yet, here was the same beat-up silver mailbox in an overgrown hedge of arbor vide.

Jay pulled up behind a Ford Bronco pickup, shut the car off and smoked a cigarette while he watched the house. When a face peeked from a window he got out of his car, and walked slowly up onto the porch and knocked. The porch boards squawked under his feet. A woman of about thirty came to the screen door in a housecoat. She gave him a quizzing look, but didn't say anything to him. She didn't seem very threatening. Ah, good, he thought, maybe I can settle this whole thing quickly with her, and get the hell out of here.

Jay said, "I've come to apologize. I suppose you've wondered who broke into your house about five years ago and stole your record player. It was me." He took some cash from his pocket. "I can pay for it, too."

She blinked and brushed her tangled brown hair back from her eyes.. "Just a minute," she said, and turned to holler, "Ed." She hollered about five times.

God, Jay thought.

When a middle-aged man stepped out onto the porch, she disappeared meekly inside. "What is it you want?" the man said. The man was wiry, and his wool socks—he was shoeless—were pulled up over the cuffs of his jeans. He was taller than Jay.

Jay explained his mission, falteringly, while the man squinted at him.

Then the man hollered, "Roberta." He hollered without actually looking back at the door, "you wanna come out here?" The woman re-emerged reluctantly, also squinting. It didn't seem to Jay that it was such a bright morning. Why all the squinting? "Explain yourself to her, will you?" the man said.

"Well, I already did," said Jay.

"He's talking about a record player," the man said,

"but I don't know what it's got to do with anything."

"It was your record player," Jay said, "your stereo or whatever."

"Oh, Ed, remember? Your mother's record player? But she come when we wasn't here and took it back."

Recognition came over the man's face. "And half my records with it, too," Now he squinted at Jay again, and pointed at his chest. "My mother send you?"

"No," Jay said. He almost laughed with exasperation. It had really been a hard morning. "I came on my own. You see, I'm in this sobriety program and I have to apologize—"

"Well, you tell that old lady something for me, will you? You tell her I said she's about as dumb as they make them. She took my records and forgot to take her own. That's what she gets for sneaking around in the dark. You hear? And you tell her I said if she wants them, she can come and get them her own self. I ain't giving you jackshit." With that the man took the woman by her shoulder and escorted her back into the house, and let the screen door swat shut.

Jay lit a cigarette on his way back to his car. Mud from the road had spattered his doors almost up to his windows. He stuffed the money back in his jeans and got in slowly, and began backing out of the driveway. Nobody gets it, he thought. He said it aloud as he drove, shaking his head. "*No*-body gets it."

Acknowledgments

First, I wish to thank Simon Pontin, morning-show host of
WXXI-FM, Rochester, New York, for granting me the forum
and air-time for my "Fiction in Shorts" radio show for which I
wrote all the stories in this volume. Although some of the stories appeared first in print, and some are substantially changed,
lengthened, and even re-titled from their radio format, "Fiction
in Shorts" provided an opportunity and inspiration to work in the
"short-short" form, or "flash fiction," as it is sometimes called. All
the stories here eventually aired, except "Cow's Eyes," which was
not broadcast because of its original length. My radio format is
four minutes, which is enough time for about 750 words.

I wish to thank the editors of the following journals in which
some of these stories first appeared in print:

"Island Goats" was first published in *Lake Affect;*

"Paris" and "The Shadow of Hollywood" in *The English Record*;

"The Grand Hotel" in *Haz-mat*;

"Latch" in the *Carlton Review*.

Thanks are also due to several people who read some of these
stories in early drafts, or listened to them on the air, and provided comments, suggestions, and much-needed encouragement:
Kurt Brown, Laure-Anne Bosselaar, Betsy Gilbert, Meg Kearney,
Rahul Mehta, and Paola Peroni.

In addition, I gratefully acknowledge permission granted to re-
print lines from the following poems:

"The Force That Through the Green Fuse Drives the Flower" (excerpt) by Dylan Thomas, from *The Poems of Dylan Thomas*, copyright © 1939 by New Directions Publishing Corp..

"Over Sir John's Hill" (excerpt) by Dylan Thomas, from *The Poems of Dylan Thomas*, copyright © 1952 by Dylan Thomas. Reprinted by permission of New Directions Publishing Corp.

About the Author

Steven Huff is the author of two full collections of poetry, *More Daring Escapes* (Red Hen Press, 2008) and *The Water We Came From* (FootHills Publishing, 2003), and a chapbook of poems, *Proof* (Two Rivers Review Press, 2004). His fiction has won a Pushcart Prize, and a story was short-listed for an O. Henry Prize in 2002. His poetry has been read on Garrison Keillor's *The Writer's Almanac* from Minnesota Public Radio. He teaches writing at Rochester Institute of Technology, and in the MFA program at Pine Manor College, and serves as director of adult education at the Writers & Books literary center, and has a weekly radio show, "Fiction in Shorts" on WXXI-FM, and WJSL-FM.